# 15

# VIEWS OF MIAMI

*Edited by Jaquria Díaz | Series Editor: Nathan Holic*

BURROW PRESS

© Burrow Press and its contributors, 2014
Illustrations by Alex Lenhoff
Book Design by Tina Craig

ISBN: 978-0-9849538-3-7
E-ISBN: 978-0-9849538-9-9
LCCN: 2014938739

Burrow Press
PO Box 533709
Orlando, FL 32853
info@burrowpress.com

Print: burrowpress.com
Web: burrowpressreview.com
Flesh: functionallyliterate.org

Distributed by Itasca Books
orders@itascabooks.com

The story "Jamokes," written for 15 Views by John
Dufresne, first appeared in *Tri-Quarterly*.

# ABOUT THE 15 VIEWS SERIES

The 15 Views series features anthologies of loosely linked fiction set in Florida as told by authors who live (or once lived) in a given city.

One author sets the sequence in motion, and the fourteen authors that follow must (1) set their stories in a new location, and (2) link their story to one of the previous by something as concrete as a character, insignificant as an object, or as abstract as a metaphor. The result is a sprawling literary portrait of a Florida city.

This series is inspired by the late Jeanne Leiby. Though she passed away on April 19, 2011, her work as an editor (at *Black Warrior Review*, *The Florida Review*, and finally at *The Southern Review*), a teacher and mentor (at Alabama, Tennessee, UCF, and LSU), and a fiction writer (the collection *Downriver*), will certainly be remembered for many years to come.

# TABLE OF CONTENTS

# MY MIAMI: THE CITY THAT GAVE ME STORIES
Jaquira Díaz

*Introduction*

As I was bringing together the fifteen authors that make up *15 Views of Miami*, my goal was to make this list as diverse as possible—writers both established and emerging, essayists and fiction writers and poets. Fifteen different voices. Some Miami natives, like Susanna Daniel, J. David Gonzalez, Jennine Capó Crucet, and Leonard Nash. Some transplants, like Patricia Engel, M.J. Fievre, and Lynne Barrett. Some who haven't lived in the city in over ten years—like Phillippe Diederich and Ian Vasquez—and some who have never left.

These stories are linked—sometimes by a character that returns in a second story, sometimes by an image or a place that appeared in a previous story, sometimes thematically. The links are often subtle, and sometimes they sneak up on you. You'll find in these pages writers and characters from different cultures, a variety of languages, of styles, of neighborhoods. You'll find ugliness and pain, but also beauty, art, ghosts, love. You'll be overcome with nostalgia and laughter and longing. And if, like me, you've spent the last four months shoveling snow in the Midwest, you'll find yourself dreaming of the sun, the ocean, scorching-hot cortaditos.

These fifteen views explore the ugly truth. They are portraits of a city in which characters are not stereotypes, not victims or villains, but flawed and human and sometimes brutal—characters who cling to their humanity even during moments of great pain, and find meaning in unexpected places. These stories are playful and evocative and multifaceted and dangerous and strange. Just like my Miami.

*

My family moved to South Beach from Puerto Rico in the '80s, before the modeling agencies and five-star restaurants, before gentrification, before the city's emergence as a gay mecca, before it became the tourist destination it is today. There was no glitz and glamour, no waiting in traffic for three hours because another action movie was being filmed on the MacArthur Causeway. In the '80s and early '90s, my neighborhood was mostly populated by Hasidic Jews, Latinos, Haitians, white-haired retirees, and the working poor who lived in the rat-infested, run-down, art deco slums. For the most part, the models and musicians and talent scouts steered clear of our neighborhood, unless they were looking to buy dope, which sometimes they were.

Back then, the Beach was under development. Real estate investors had started buying and renovating the art deco apartment buildings and historic hotels that had flourished during the Beach's golden years. And while we lived in a place where money was revitalizing an entire city, we were poor. We lived within walking distance of Flamingo Park, where I played basketball with the neighborhood kids, hung out in the public pool, tagged all over the piss-soaked handball courts. My father worked two jobs, seven days a week, barely managing to support a family of five. We were always behind on rent. Every month our phone was disconnected. We never had cable. We sometimes lived without electricity. My brother and I took turns killing the mice that lived in the hole behind the fridge, whacking them with our abuela's cast-iron skillet. We were grateful for free school lunches, sometimes our only meal of the day. We went without air conditioning in the summer, without heat in the winter, without mousetraps ever.

This was not the Miami Beach most people know. This was the Miami of *Cocaine Cowboys*, during the Drug Wars, and shootouts in the street were a real thing. Most of us back then knew someone—or knew *of* someone—who had been marked by violence. Everyone had these stories: a kid they'd known from the neighborhood, a kid they'd grown up with, barely seventeen, who'd been shot outside a nightclub. A boy they'd been on a date with, killed by some gang members, his head cracked open with a metal pipe. I also had these stories: an uncle who was stabbed in front of a crowd while at a salsa concert in Calle Ocho, a friend who was stabbed in a street fight and ended up in Jackson Memorial Hospital with a collapsed lung. Growing up in Miami, I saw these stories multiply. There would be another friend stabbed in a fight, a boyfriend's best friend killed in a drive-by shooting when we were barely fourteen, a classmate's brother shot in the face, a girl I'd known since third grade found murdered in her bathroom.

We learned to live with these things. We assumed that this was the way the world worked—some of us lived, some of us died. Even if we were just bystanders. Even if we were just kids.

Over the years, I've scoured many bookshelves in search of my Miami—a Miami where people of all races and cultures and backgrounds and languages are the main characters, not just sidekicks or criminals or Others, not just caricatures, but people with flaws and dreams and desires. As a kid, even when I was fighting or playing basketball or skipping school to spend the day at the beach, I read voraciously. I read everything I could get my hands on—*Dracula*, *To Kill a Mockingbird*, *The Catcher in the Rye*, *Lord of the Flies*, and whatever else the Miami Beach librarian put in my hands—but I never saw myself in books. The stories I read were full of adventure, vampires, heroes, mystery, murder, and characters who were nothing like me, who didn't share my experience, or my background, or my language, or my *anything*. It was clear that these writers weren't writing with me in mind, or people who looked like me and loved like me, who lived in neighborhoods like mine. So I started writing for me.

I wrote terrible stories and screenplays, mostly rewrites of movies like *Back to the Future*, *The Neverending Story*, and *The Goonies*. Except in my versions, the protagonists were always nine-year-old Puerto Rican girls traveling through time, or singing "Twist and Shout" at a Puerto Rican festival in Bayfront Park, or saving Wynwood from pirates. These girls were from my Miami, and they kicked some serious ass. And for some mysterious reason, they were always named Maria.

As I look back at all my Marias, I realize I was writing them out of necessity. The Marias were my way of revising these worlds where people like me were invisible, where my Miami didn't exist.

Over the years, I lived in several Miami neighborhoods: South Beach, North Beach, Normandy Isles, North Miami, Miami Shores, East Hialeah, West Hialeah, Kendall. I've left Miami half a dozen times, but I keep coming back. It's a strange city—never the same place for long. It's always changing, evolving, reinventing itself. The Miami Beach of my childhood and adolescence is long gone: Nautilus Middle School and Miami Beach High were completely demolished, new buildings erected in their place. Rolo's Restaurant, where I held my very first job? Gone. With the gentrification of Miami Beach, once-famous landmarks like Wolfie's, The Fontainebleau, The Carillon, and Penrod's are now either gone or "renovated" for a different clientele, low-income families and the working-class displaced. Since the beginning of this project, Shuckers Bar & Grill, the setting of Corey Ginsberg's "In Plain Sight," closed down due to an unfortunate accident: the waterfront deck collapsed, injuring at least two dozen people. We still don't know if there will be a reopening. Yes, the narrative of my Miami is sometimes sad, but there is also growth, progress, and, of course, a plethora of stories.

# ONCE
Ricardo Pau-Llosa
*Wynwood Arts District*

Eleven o'clock was Chato's favorite hour. It generated a crest-of-wave lift then drop into the enduring mundane which others saved for the zodiacal minute of their first-born. Chato could be glimpsed smiling at his watch any time after 10:30 AM so as to not miss the roll and pass. He could always tell when it was eleven, watch or no watch. Chato, the snub-nosed, oddly noticeable short guy, was a romantic, he told himself, which is why he yearned to produce wine, in his Miami-Cuban factory, polyester, plastic-covered furniture hometown of Hialeah.

"Ay, Chato," his mother would say to him as a boy, and *Ay Chato* would echo in his bulldog of a mind. The sigh of destiny: first professional basketball player of a certain height, a Nobel in this or that, a billionaire with a harem of models whose legs began at his ears, a speed record. In his mid-forties, no siblings, wife, or children, parents dead, Chato dodged a bottle of beer during a break-up with a fiancée when it occurred to him to pursue wine-making and make Hialeah the Rioja of Florida. No data about climate or soil could rend the curtain on this, his sober surrender to mission.

And what else could Chato call his wine but "Once," which in Spanish means "eleven" but in English captures the wistful passion for re-puzzled pasts which drove his mother into a labyrinth of society-gossip magazines from a Cuba that died half a century ago. Chato conjured the advertising slogans and was pleasantly unsurprised to notice that the best ideas came to him around his favorite hours of the day. "Once There Were Eleven" was the one he settled on. Vaguely allusive to mystical twelves, it captured dualities he felt native. Was the bottle the twelfth entity that would complete the consumer's happiness? He discarded the slogans he knew the advertisers would cherish, Once Upon a Wine, and in Spanish, *Once onzas de oro para beber* (eleven ounces of gold to drink). But as he dreamed of a great harvest, within him stirred the hairy back of guilt. These ploys disguised, even denied, the fervor which led him to dream of a Hialeah wine. Is it brave to nurture passions no one else could respect?

Chato had not taken the first step in planting a vineyard, not even learning the fine art of winemaking, and already he saw himself on the cover of magazines, clinking glasses with celebrities, receiving the swoons of a thirsty world. At first he thought this was the wave effect of the eleventh hour. The number was, after all, a double-code that celebrates the uniqueness of firsts. Eleven is also a vertical equal sign, the two rungs of a ladder that embody an infinite pattern, indeed all patterns—stairs and marching soldiers and braided hair, spirals and drumbeats, chords and painted geometries, chopsticks that turn into mandalas. Individuals facing each other as equals in a duel or in love. Chato realized that his wine would make all this clear, even urgent, to folks everywhere. It wasn't the number that would make the wine, but the wine that would make the number.

After four months our dreamer had only managed to assemble some of the vats and instruments. The vineyard would rise on the shore of the nameless canal that split Hialeah from Miami to the south, a straight-edged extension that linked the Miami River to the Everglades, all the way up to Lake Okeechobee in mid-peninsula. *Vino Once* would christen Hialeah's Grand Canal. But the words kept entangling him, much as the canals the US Army Corps of Engineers had dug through the Glades to regulate water flow and now caged the wetlands in straight lines. A rectilinear fingerprint, Chato mused as he googled a map of the region, curious to see where these blue strings came from and where they ended. He'd wrap his wine in a blue wire basket. "Vino Once" could be Spanglish for "He Came Once," or bad Spanish for "Eleven Came," or with missing words "He Came at Eleven." Hialeah was the language butcher-shop while Miami was trying to hop on the global glamour train like an agile hobo. It was at 10:59 PM on a Tuesday in August when Chato realized he would open his storefront in the Wynwood Arts District and launch his brand on the opening night of the December fairs.

"*Ay, Chato, Chato*," his brick-layer father would say to him as a boy, "*tú siempre te las buscas.*" Was Chato really always getting himself in trouble he didn't need? Did his father mean that Chato would always get what he wants and find his way out of problems? Ambiguity haunted him from birth, and that no doubt led him to his love for Eleven. "*Chato en camisa de once varas*," his father would say every time the old man had to bail him out of a crisis. What a clever saying, Chato thought, an eleven-yard shirt to describe troubles one could have avoided. My wine will instead be the flat golden land of grain and marshes from which flocks rise in white unison over the trains bursting with barrels of *Once*. Chato would tower over those petty *mayameros* bereft of undulance.

By early fall the buzz of the fairs was mounting and Chato got to work. He rented a Wynwood storefront near 29$^{th}$ Street and Miami Avenue, where the fairs mushroom in their white, block-wide, air-conditioned tents on weedy fields surrounded by the quilt of sleek galleries and dumpy workshops that proliferate in the District. Deco café tables around a green marble-top curvaceous bar, and behind it teak racks for three hundred wine bottles. The slanted cradles swirled with the grains of tropical trees, all awaiting the bottles of ecstasy. Wiry lamps dangled like tungsten spiders against the burgundy and pumice grey walls. *Vino Once* was decked out for the crowds, but where was the wine? Chato had been raised to believe one had to work backwards from the goal to the original cause, lest the desired end escape like a bird from its cage at any point in the process.

One Saturday, as the workmen were wrapping up, Chato was surprised to see, standing on the sidewalk, a beautiful woman he found vaguely familiar. She cupped her left hand over her forehead to block out the sun and gaze upon the sign. Then she looked with delighted curiosity into the shop and crept in, asking if it was okay, and the workers said yeah, sure, at the tanned legs.

"Chato!" she screamed.

"Pica!" he screamed back, as they embraced. "*Tanto tiempo.*"

They pulled up chairs on the floor still sprinkled with sawdust and electric wire clippings. The workers kept their rhythm but listened in on the conversation. They knew for sure now Chato had money. They should have charged him more. How did gorgeous get that nickname? the workers asked themselves beneath the hammer blows and ladder racket and the chewing of rancid gum. Was Pica itchy? Was she the type to pick a guy's wallet clean, like the bird she seemed?

"But what's all this, Chato? Are you importing wine now? *Divino.*" And she chuckled, catching her own pun.

"*Bueno*, Pica, you know I've always liked to do things my way. I am making this wine, the *Vino de Hialeah*." And he paused to let the name out like a sigh. "*Once*, which the *americanos* read as 'once upon a time.'"

Pica looked at him the way a fish does into a mirror, with a bewilderment she knew she could neither fake nor shake. She didn't know how to ask him the indelicate questions about where he learned to make wine, and where he was making it, and where he was growing grapes in this muggy wet. So, to fill the silence, Chato went on.

"When the fairs open, I'm going to throw a bash, with wine for everyone's tasting. *¿Qué te parece?*"

"What do I think? I told you, *divino*. I have to go, but just one question. Why the name *Once?*"

Chato figured the time was right to flirt. After all, Pica looked great, much slimmer now than twelve years ago when they dated briefly but passionately. "*Mira*, Pica, it's a reference to size, you know. Eleven… Remember?" His grin filled in the rest.

"Not even centimeters." Pica bounced up a swirl of construction dust as she left. The workers held their laughter until she exited.

*

It was the big night of the fairs. Chato bought a few bottles of imported spirits and put up a poster of the forthcoming *Vino Once*, the pride of Hialeah. But the van carrying the wines crashed on the way, and by opening time there was not a drop of vino in the store. The refugees from the openings across the street assembled. Their anticipation grew amid the store's appointments. Pica showed up with her current boyfriend, a painter who was having a solo show in one of the fairs. Athletic, tall, ponytail and earring. Realizing the eleven-yard shirt Chato had gotten himself into, Pica asked her lover to plop her onto the counter where she could address the crowd.

"*Señores y señoras*, everybody, listen to me." The crowd hushed and turned to her. "How do you like my debut as an artist?" She waved her right arm pointing to the empty racks. "Yes, this is a conceptual piece titled 'Once There Was Wine.' It's an installation I've set up in the guise of a store that sells invisible wine. You all know how everyone dreams empty dreams in Miami, and makes up stories about their past. This is my statement about the empty rituals of our time and place." She paused to feed their amazement. "Martí said of Cuba that our wine was sour, but it is our wine, and I'm saying our wine in Miami is invisible, so drink up!"

Everyone clapped. Some teared up. A new conceptual artist had emerged in their very midst. Chato felt grateful to Pica for saving him from a disastrous dive into certain ridicule, but he also felt usurped. Pica had turned this failed dream into her own fantasy. Pica's boyfriend, Bruno, was miffed. This art world groupie had used him, he figured, to launch herself. Already there were a few dealers and curators who wanted to speak with her about her career. "Miami's Emptiness Gets a Resounding Voice," the review headlines would read.

Pica made her way back to the fairs. Bruno and Chato sat in the now empty store like two bottles kicked across the floor. Slowly, as they recovered from Pica's swoop into their dreams, each one began to think of the other as the architect of this ambush. Did Chato conspire with Pica to get her back? Did Bruno give Pica this idea to pay him back for dumping her twelve years ago? Or maybe just to humiliate him, so Pica would never think of coming back to Chato? In ways that only deepened his anxiety, Chato thought of them both as the two 1s in the number eleven. He envied and desired Bruno's heartless simplicity.

Bruno was the first to break the silence, as he slowly got up from his chair. "As the Germans say, *einmal ist keinmal.*" He translated for numb Chato, "One time is no time."

Chato guessed it meant, *un mal no es un mal*—one bad thing is not a bad thing. He relished the ambiguities. Could this be the name of a product that would make the world turn and love him? Bruno stood like a bronze warrior before Chato, who was slumped in his chair, holding his head up with both elbows.

A melted cheese of a man, thought Bruno, who imagined the winemaker's soul lapping onto the floor in eleven yards of blobs and folds.

# ANGELS OF EDEN
## Phillippe Diederich
### *Homestead*

We came into Homestead on a cold December night. The following day we found work at Eden Farms picking yellow squash and cucumber. It got so cold that first week, we thought the crop would freeze and worried the trip had been a waste of time and money. Every morning we started at dawn, covered in layers of clothes we'd picked up at the Goodwill on Campbell Drive, and worked our rows, bodies stooped like hunchbacks, slicing the plants with little curved knives, the cold like needles on our fingertips.

When we got paid at the end of the month, Jacinto and you and I went to La Morenita store to buy phone cards and to send money to our people back in Guerrero. This was before my mother passed away, before anyone knew she had the cancer. But I could tell something was wrong because when we spoke on the telephone her breathing was so heavy, it was as if she were forcing her breath through her *huipil*.

"She sounds," I said to Jacinto as we walked back to the trailer, "as if she's whispering secrets."

That was the day we saw *la niña* standing at the end of the shopping plaza in front of La Frontera. She was young, maybe fifteen, and had pretty black eyes, and her hair was braided in a long tight *trensa* down the length of her back with no ribbon.

"*Irala*," Jacinto said and grabbed his crotch. "She looks lost. Maybe I should show her the way, *no?*"

I said nothing. In her eyes I had seen a sad gentleness so pure it wrinkled my heart.

We bunked in a narrow apartment that stank of urine and corn, eleven of us, all men, all in our late teens, all of us from *pueblos* and villages in Guerrero and Oaxaca that nobody knew existed. On Sunday after church we went to the Coin Laundry and the Winn Dixie, and in the afternoon we built a fire in the rusted grill someone had abandoned between the rows of apartments. We grilled meat and drank cans of Bud Lite and sat in the sun. That's when I wandered. At first I didn't know I was seeking *la niña*. I just roamed along the dark streets of Homestead like a stray, thinking of my people back home. I had a *prometida,* a girl who had been promised to me back in my *pueblo*, but this *niña* had done something to me. Like a *bruja*, she wouldn't leave my mind.

The first time she spoke to me, it was outside La Tropical market. She said something about Christmas. Something terribly sad got a hold of me that afternoon as I walked her to the front of the apartments by the railroad tracks, across the street from the recycling place. She touched my arm so gently it sent a cold shiver up my tailbone.

And then one day after a long day in the field, I saw her outside Doris Beauty Supply. I was dirty and stinking of sweat and the chemicals they spray in the field, but she waved at me to come.

"What happened to you, *pues?*" I said. She had long red welts on the back of her neck and cheek.

She told me about her life in Homestead and how she worked the *pizca* in the field like everyone else, but also cooked and cleaned for her brother and the other men who lived in the apartment with them. "And sometimes," she said in a voice so delicate it reminded me of the dewdrops that collected on the petals of the wildflowers that bloomed in my *pueblo*. "My brother's *compadre* tries to sneak into my bed. But I fight him. Every time I fight him. No matter how tired I am I fight. I kick. I hit. I use my fists, clenched. He says he loves me, wants to marry me."

"Did you tell your brother?" I asked.

"He's a drunk just like the rest of those *canijos.*"

But not me. I was not like any of them. I had to show her. So every night I left our apartment, tired and beat from the day's labor, and wandered the long flat streets of Homestead like a ghost in the dark while everyone else stayed inside the walls of the two rooms, talking, sleeping, dreaming of home, of our sisters and our mothers and all that we'd left in our *pueblos*, the dry valleys and the steep mountains that smelled of pine and mud.

We had talked of many things, but I never told her of my *prometida*. When I think of it now, it seems odd how much I talked about my *prometida* when I first arrived in this country. I bragged about her when we worked, when I slept. But I never talked about *la niña* to Jacinto or anyone else. Even in my dreams I was silent like a stone. That month, all I could think of was how she made my insides feel as if a storm were raging inside me. All this I understood because in Homestead the moon rose like a second sun, pale and powerful in its mystery. I watched it through the ripped screen of the window as I lay on the mattress on the floor of the apartment. The moon was as brutal as the weight we carried, the weight of leaving our homes to come North. The homesickness never leaves you. It's an open scar running the length of your chest, and all you can do is numb it with liquor.

One week, after we got paid, we saw her by the Boost, a store where we bought phone cards and sent money. She cupped her left hand over her forehead to block out the sun. When I came closer I saw her eye was black and her hair a mess. She didn't come up to me that time. She just eyed us suspiciously. Then she disappeared around the corner. I followed.

Later, I told Jacinto I had to help her. "She's in a bad place," I said. "I have to."

"But what can you do?" Jacinto spoke the truth. "You have nothing."

Late that night I packed my bag, took all my money and left the apartment. I thought we would catch a bus, go to another town. People said there was always work in Immokalee, or from there we could just go north and work the oranges. It didn't matter. We were going away together, and that's all I could think about. We met in the fields of Eden Farms and she hugged me between the rows of dead squash, the moon staring down at us like a wide silver eye.

"So we're leaving," she said, her tone broken like a promise. "For real?"

I dropped my bag in the soft dirt and took her in my arms and pressed my lips against hers. They were tender and liquid, and I felt myself turning into air, gliding up to the moon until the men fell upon me with blows from broken broom sticks and clenched fists and work-boots like stones.

\*

They took everything: my money, my bag, my clothes, and even the snakeskin boots I'd bought in Amarillo when I first arrived in this country and we were working our way up to Oregon for the *pizca* of the cherries.

That's when the angels came. A dozen lanky angels, black and shining like polished leather in the moonlight. They danced and spoke in tongues and lifted me high in the air like a sad cloud. I thought I was dead. When I opened my eyes I was in a small room that smelled of cumin and clove. A black woman with a scarf like peacock feathers on her head fed me pumpkin soup. She healed the cut on my face and applied a balm to the bruises on my sides and back. She told me she had learned to speak Spanish at a *batey* in the Dominican Republic when she was married to her second husband. "*Un perro.*" She laughed, pronouncing the Rs like Ls so it sounded as if she'd said "hair," not "dog."

And then she shared the wisdom of how everyone dreams empty dreams in places like Homestead and Miami, and makes up stories about their past. "This is my statement about the empty rituals of our time and place," she said, but I had no idea what she meant. I still don't.

This story I told you in pieces, Fernando. I told you as I remembered the moments that connect the thread of my life. Months later, when we were planting onions in Colorado and I got the news that my mother had passed away, we spent the night in a hotel under the interstate. We got drunk on cheap tequila and got tattoos. You had your family name written like a flash of glory across your chest: Gonzalez. I had the *Virgen de Guadalupe* behind my left shoulder. "For protection," I said. "To keep me on the straight and narrow until I get home."

But by then even I could tell my voice was resigned. Something bitter clung to the vowels when I spoke, like I was angry at the world, holding a grudge for all the misfortunes it had handed me. I couldn't tell if it was for my mother or *la niña* or my *prometida* back home, or just because I had finally discovered the world had its own order, and that no matter how hard I worked or how much I tried, I would always be crawling in the dirt, that I would never see *la niña*, or go back to Homestead in this lifetime.

# IMELDA'S LULLABY
## M. Evelina Galang
### *Coral Gables*

She lies on a cot at the foot of the old woman's bed, the air con humming just under La Doña's snoring respirator. Across the room, the curtains blow just high enough to reveal a sliver of the moon. Imelda squints, wishes Manila were outside that window, not Miami.

La Doña is thick-boned and fat and so still that, even with the machine, Imelda rises, just to check. She places her small hand on the old one's belly, lets it rest until she feels La Doña's breath, the fall and rise of it steady and deep. Asleep like this, dead like this, there is something beautiful about the old one. The lines on her face smooth away like creases on silken sheets, and the cheekbones rise high and regal. The mouth, hidden under the mask, is set in its eternal pout. La Doña insists on lipstick. "What if there's emergency in the middle of the night? ¿Y mi cara? Fea." Even sleeping she is difficult, Imelda thinks. Plastic rollers and thick black bobby pins circle the old woman's face like a magnificent pink halo.

Awake, the old woman's fea comes out. She screams fast Spanish, swallows her consonants and spews bits of chewed up food at Imelda. La Doña, malcriada widow, living alone at the edge of the Gables, her children scattered like seed—New York, San Francisco, Chicago. Not a single one fallen close to this old tree. This vieja reminds Imelda of her Ate Remedios, the spinster lola never able to keep her nurses. They run away on her. Climb the iron gates and slip across borders like butiki in the night.

Tao yoon, she told her ate once. Why make them sleep on floors?

They are help, her aunt answered. Hindi familia. Hindi kaibigan. I pay them to work. Beds are for guests.

*

Imelda wipes La Doña's brow. At least you give me a cot, she whispers. From inside, a breath escapes, deep and low like a secret. On nights like these, she thinks about the other side of this life, where it is daylight and the city is thick with traffic. Cocks are crowing and she wakes to the melody of a lullaby, soft and low and floating like wind. Sunlight surrounds the house, then fills it with the noise of the city.

Back home, Imelda was the youngest beauty of three daughters, in a house of maids and cooks and drivers. Her mother taught the sisters how to direct the cook, the labandera, the katulong who scrubbed the floors. She went to all-girl convent schools and never talked to boys, though she knew they were watching. And by the time she was 20, she married Armando Chin, a businessman who owned an air con factory. He was ambitious and worked long hours. He gave her a house in Makati with marble floors and terraces filled with sweet sampaguita blossoms. They raised a beautiful family. He gave her everything. I was always too nice, she thinks.

La Doña spits up thick mucus and Imelda leaps to her bedside, holding the mask off the bitter face and gently washing with a damp towel. The old body seizes, then crumples up like used tissue.

"Leave me, China!" she shouts.

"Espere, señora," Imelda says.

"¡Pare!" Her arms rise up like two legs walking. The hand sprawls fat and lush. The red fingernails try to dig into Imelda's light skin.

"Tranquila," she tells the old woman. "Or I will sing."

Imelda holds her breath, but the sour smell of the dying seeps past her, soaks into her own skin. And still she washes little rivers of vomit that have trickled down La Doña's chin. Wipes the perspiration from her own brow.

"Did my son call?" asks La Doña.

"No, señora."

"¿Y mi hija—los dos?"

"No, señora."

La Doña might have been an old spinster. The phone in the house never rings.

"What do you know," La Doña hisses. "You're not even a nurse."

"No, señora, I'm not. But I am all you have."

"Cheap help."

"Your only help."

"Illegal help, China."

Imelda ignores the insults, though her Spanish is nearly excellent. Instead she thinks, Holy Mary, Mother of God, pray for us. She sings to the old woman. And that's when she sees La Doña has wet her bedding.

*

When Imelda found the letters, she threw his things out the balcony—didn't even bother to bag the laundry, to box the toiletries, to unplug his clocks and stereo and speakers. Those things she yanked from the walls and hurled onto their terrace patio to crash and break and scatter.

He cut her off. He cut the children off. He told her she had grown soft and plain and matronly. "What did you think I would do?" he asked her.

How could she have missed this? Fifteen years.

She found a job in the Ayala Museum and fed the children herself. She spent money on them as if he were still in the house. Margarita went to the beauty parlor twice a week to have her coarse hair blow-dried for one thousand pesos each visit. Jun-Jun partied with his barcada at swanky clubs and hotels in Makati. She held on to the help.

"Mahirap kami," she told the cook. She paid her a little less and started washing dishes.

"Please ma'am. Don't. Nakakahiya."

"Please. Kitchen ko. I am the one who is embarrassed."

She gave the maids weekends off and learned to wash the laundry.

*

"Don't handle me like that, China," snaps the old lady. "I'm not a baby."

"Permiso, señora," she answers, head bowed, eyes down. But inside she thinks, and yet you soil yourself as if you are.

Imelda must bend her knees and take a breath to roll the old woman to her side, to pull the sheets out from under her, wash her backside dry. "Let me clean you first and then we'll sit up."

"It's the middle of the night, China."

"Just for a while. Until I change the bedding."

"You'd think they'd check on me—just once or twice. Me estoy muriendo."

"You are not dying."

"¿Eres médica?" Silence. "I didn't think so, China."

It isn't just the urine, the pale yellow of human stink rising from wet sheets, it's the smell of decay, of breath fermented by the night. Imelda rolls the body bit by bit, singing softly to herself, turning the backside, the torso, the shoulders. She washes the vieja with her right hand, with her elbow, with her whole body, and with the other arm, she holds her up.

"China, you're too small to handle this."

"I can handle this. I do, don't I?"

"Faster, China. I'm cold."

La Doña's body is a fat loaf of unbaked bread, oozing from her frame, and under this moonlight it appears to be rising fast with yeast. Imelda closes her eyes.

*

Because she loved her children more than anything, because she couldn't let them know the truth—they were poor and their father had abandoned them, not for work but for a second family—because there was nothing else to do when Jun-Jun showed up bruised and begging after weeks of gambling, she borrowed four million pesos to pay off Jun-Jun's losses, to afford Magarita's lifestyle at the Rockwell, to pay for her tourist visa and to arrive here in the United States of America as Mrs. Armando Chin. She let her visa lapse. Went into hiding and waited. When she heard about La Doña she considered the job a blessing, a secret to fix her problems. Dollar to pesos, she'd make the money back in months, she thought. She considered the alternatives—to turn to Armando and beg, to admit defeat to her elders, to marry a rich old white tourist, to sell everything they owned, and worst of all, to refuse Margarita and Jun-Jun—but none of it made sense to her. Always too nice, is what Ate Remedios told her.

"You let those children walk all over you. You spoil them."

"I love them, Ate. It's not their fault."

"And what about Armando? What is he doing that others are not? Naive, too."

Imelda was different than her sisters. Her sisters married well too, but they never befriended their katulong. They never apologized for anything. Once, her ate invited her husband's cariñosa to their eldest daughter's wedding.

"Why not," her ate told her. "She has a husband too. And a reputation. Why make a scene."

\*

"Cuidado, China! I am old. I break!"

Imelda lifts the old woman from the bed, heaves her gently onto two feet and shifts her into the wheelchair. "This will only take a moment," she says.

"I am not a baby," says the old woman, struggling as Imelda straps her in and places a soft flannel blanket over her knees.

"Do you want to fall?"

"Are you never in a bad mood?" When Imelda doesn't answer, the old woman snorts. "Me molesta, China."

"Do you want to sleep on dirty sheets?"

She peels the soiled linen from the bed, her hands gracing the wet stains. The smell suffocates her. The curtains blow up. The glittery moon—thin like a fingernail, hooked like a sly smile—is running fast away from her.

"What happened to your husband, China? To your children? Why aren't you with them?"

"Can't you see I'm working? Your children treat me well."

"They pay you well, you mean. You don't fool me, China. Something bad happened. No?"

"You and el señor left Cuba."

"We had no choice."

"So then, we are the same, ma'am."

"Maybe you are running."

*

Every minute since she arrived her life with La Doña is a series of castigations, war dances, word battles of the mind. It doesn't matter, Imelda thinks. She's old and she has no one else. Even if she figured it out, she wouldn't turn her in.

Every month, Imelda wires money to the children. Some of it for their living expenses, some to pay off the loan. She sends the money to Jun-Jun and, in this way, she makes her way home little bit by little bit. Five years now and it seems the U.S. dollars are barely making a dent, but she keeps working. What else is she to do?

She takes a deep breath and hoists La Doña back into her bed. She takes the curlers out of her hair one by one.

"But it isn't daylight," says the old one.

"You should rest now, with your head to the pillow." She brushes the brittle curls out and runs her fingers over the old woman's scalp. She sings just under her breath.

"Louder," says La Doña. "If you're going to sing, then sing."

The melody comes out of her like waves pushing gently through the ocean. The stars come out like children, watching the old woman waft into a deep sleep. This is the song she sang to her own boy and girl, cradled in her arms, dancing in the middle of the night. La Doña's eyes close. She takes a deep breath and slowly sleep comes.

*

The morning is dark. The moon lights through the window. The phone rings and wakes Imelda. The voice at the other end of the line, distant and cutting in and out, is crying. There has been a death.

"Paano?" she asks.

"Is it for me?" calls the old woman from the bed.

Imelda holds her breath. Listens. "He lost all of it?"

"Is it my son?"

She cradles the phone in her neck. She brushes the tears away. "Sige," she says. "I have to go."

And when she returns to the old woman, she tells her it's nothing. She fluffs the pillows and straightens her comforter. "Wrong number," she says.

And when La Doña's eyes close again, she slips out of the house and sits under the waning moon, deep in the green of La Doña's tropical garden. She listens to the palm trees rustling—hush, hush, hush. She breathes the air—humid and soft like home. She understands now she can never go back.

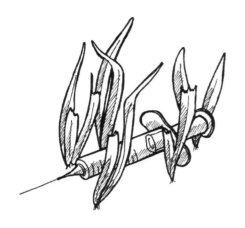

# THE JUNGLE
## Melanie Neale
### *North Miami Beach / Aventura*

Now that Maule Lake Marina had shut down and there were no dockage fees to worry about, Deal was free to focus entirely on day-to-day survival games. And if you looked at them as just that—games—they didn't seem like a drag at all. The few boats in the lake belonged either to nobodies like Deal or were simply derelict vessels with expired registrations. The registration numbers on Deal's boat had expired under the prior owner, but Deal didn't see a need to renew them.

He got up when the cabin inside his tiny sailboat got too hot for him to sleep anymore and then paddled his kayak ashore to the urban jungle.

He'd left the marina and dropped anchor near where the Oleta River fed into the lake. This put him technically in North Miami Beach waters, but since the lake was split between the towns of North Miami Beach and Aventura, local law enforcement weren't really sure how to patrol it or what, if any, the anchoring regulations were. So they left him alone.

Deal was fine with being a nobody. *La Niña* had screwed him over, but she'd taught him something too. He'd come to Miami from Indiana with his camera and his rollerblades, fresh out of film school and planning to shoot a documentary on migrant workers in Homestead. He was attracted to the simplicity of their lives—the nobility of manual labor. *La Niña*, with her dark curls and night-eyes promised to teach him what life was like for the migrants. But her brother didn't trust the white guy with the strange accent and the expensive camera, so she told Deal that they would have to meet at night and sneak onto the farms, where he could interview her in the dark. He liked the idea of this—the story of illegal workers being told in broken English by this beautiful girl, and all of the footage shot in the strange darkness of Homestead, close enough to Miami for the electric glow to creep across the fields and close enough to the Everglades for the glow to clash with pure darkness. Their first two sessions went well, but on the third he was hit from behind by something hard, and there was just enough light from the Miami glow for him to see *La Niña* scuttling through the scrub and away from him like a grotesque and smiling palmetto bug. When he woke up, he was lying in the dirt and his camera and wallet and watch were gone.

Deal didn't go to the police. He wasn't sure why he even needed a driver's license, and he didn't own the camera——MasterCard owned it, just like the government owned his expensive education. This, he realized, was the opportunity he'd been waiting for. He sat on the already-hot earth and watched the sky lighten. He was free. He walked to his Honda, which was owned by a bank as well, and then drove it to the efficiency he was renting on a month-to-month basis. He piled his clothes and laptop into the car and left the room keys in the office. He pawned his laptop, which was also owned by MasterCard, so the cash was all profit. He kept his rollerblades.

He lived in his car and washed dishes for cash in a restaurant in Coral Gables (perfect, since the government couldn't touch it). When that job ended, he moved to another one in Coconut Grove. Then a regular at the restaurant's bar offered to trade his sailboat for Deal's car. He took the trade without a pause.

Fucking *La Niña*, he thought. But he was grateful to her, too. Without her, he wouldn't be here, traipsing through the urban jungle of Greynolds Park and looking for whatever was going to make him enough money to buy dinner and a six-pack of beer for the night. Sometimes he cut behind the ABC store and crossed 163rd Street into the Oleta River State Park, but the state park tended to be full of fitness freaks on mountain bikes. The best he ever did there was to pick up a dropped piece of jewelry or a dollar bill or two. Today, he'd cover the area closer to the water and in the corner of land that was all jungle but didn't belong to either park. There were very few rules here. Part encampment and part unadulterated Florida nature, it was an area where he might disturb a great blue heron with one step and crush a used hypodermic with the next.

It was cool in the shade of Australian pines and mangroves. Deal didn't talk to the inhabitants of the jungle because, in his heart, he knew he wasn't like them. Sure, he was off the grid. But he had a home. His little boat. He didn't have electricity or running water or anything like that, but he had a home. He didn't use drugs. He wasn't an addict. He smiled at the inhabitants and nodded at them but avoided them when he could.

Today, his plan was to find one of the sad men who came to the jungle at lunch. He, like the other opportunists, sat just behind the tree line near the ABC store's parking lot. There was a closed-down restaurant next to the ABC store, and the parking lot was expansive enough so that the men could park in the back, as far from Biscayne Boulevard as possible. They could don cheap shades and, slouched and glancing over their shoulders, wander into the jungle where Deal and the others would be waiting. Today, Deal watched a soft-looking one with a wedding band and an expensive watch shuffle across the parking lot. He looked safe and harmless so Deal waited for him to enter the jungle and then made eye contact. Deal turned and headed deeper into the mangroves and the man followed. Safe was a relative term. But Deal figured that married men, family-looking men, were more likely to be cautious and clean.

In the darker and deeper shadows of the jungle, the man unbuckled his belt and handed Deal some cash. Deal felt his own bare knees sink into the spongy ground as he cupped the man's balls in one hand and guided his dick into his mouth with the other.

The man stared at the pines, and Deal finished and spit and didn't follow as the man wandered back out of the jungle. He folded the cash and slid it into his pocket. He considered going to look for another man but didn't. He couldn't let himself get greedy. Greed was what had gotten him into debt in the first place. Greed and the desire to get an education. Who the fuck went to film school? He thought about how he used to rollerblade around Bloomington looking for anything interesting to catch on film, about how the angles and the speed of rollerblading made his footage bumpy and surreal. Now everything was surreal. Life was as fucking surreal as anything he'd ever caught on camera.

Deal spent the rest of the afternoon with his eyes on the jungle floor, wandering through the pines and mangroves looking for anything that may have fallen out of a man's pocket during a lunchtime transaction. He picked up some quarters and a five and called it a day. He crossed Biscayne to the small Italian Market called Laurenzo's, where he bought a sandwich and biscotti and a six pack of expensive beer, then returned to the jungle and sat by the water and watched the mangrove snappers ghost through the shallows. He thought about buying a fishing pole but he didn't like fish all that much. And a fishing pole was one more piece of material excess that he didn't really want. The snappers surfaced periodically to gulp the bugs that skirted the surface of the water, and Deal watched them until he fell asleep on the cushion of Australian pine needles.

It was cool enough to head back to the boat when he woke up. He guessed that it was around 6 PM, because the sound of traffic on Biscayne Boulevard had increased to a vibrant humming and honking and skidding and stopping and going. He tapped the rhythm of the traffic out on his knee for a few minutes before picking up the remaining half-sandwich and three beers and cutting towards the mangrove bight where he stashed his kayak.

He slid the kayak into the water and paddled through the quiet mangroves and out to the lake. It was clear enough to see the rocks and roots and debris in the shallows, but it grew brown and cloudy as the water deepened. He preferred the rhythm of the paddles——lifting and dipping and barely causing a ripple in the glassy water——to the rhythm of the traffic on Biscayne Boulevard. He hummed along with it.

The guttural sound of a large outboard engine snapped him out of his groove and he looked up towards the lake. This was when he noticed that his sailboat was not anchored in its spot anymore. He spotted it, nearly half a mile away, tethered behind a center-console boat with the Florida Fish and Wildlife Commission emblem displayed on its hull. Both were headed for the canal that led out of the lake and into the Intracoastal Waterway. The FWC boat's motors grumbled as the uniformed driver throttled forward and the duo picked up speed. Other boats that had been anchored in the lake were gone as well, as if the FWC had chosen today to pick up the derelicts.

"Hey!" Deal raised his arms and waved as he shouted. He tried to stand in the kayak but his feet and his knees moved in two different directions as the flimsy hull wobbled and he landed back in the seat. "Hey! That's my boat!" He lifted the paddle up over his head and swung it back and forth. The uniformed driver of the FWC boat and another large man chatted and seemed to be laughing about something as they continued towards the canal, pulling Deal's boat. They both glanced at their tow as if to make sure it was still there and resumed their chatting.

Deal howled. He raised his voice higher than he'd ever raised it and banged the paddle against the hull of his kayak. A heron screamed and took off from the mangroves and the traffic on Biscayne Boulevard kept beating out its urban rhythm. Deal howled and screamed but the men never heard him. The outboard engines grew quiet as the boats entered the canal, and Deal watched the mast of his sailboat disappear behind a tall condominium building that hadn't been updated since the seventies. He watched the trail of foam and ripples that the two boats had left on the water flatten out and melt back into the smooth and glassy lake. He opened his mouth to howl again, but a loud sob came out and he slumped into his kayak and cried.

# MORNING GLORIES
## Lynne Barrett
*Upper Eastside*

*Saturday, 9:45 AM*

Sharon steps out her back door into Miami midwinter, the air so clear and sweet it should be sipped. By her back gate, the morning glories she planted after Christmas have twined up her homemade trellis, unfolding heart-shaped leaves. Now, the vines' pale tips lift, seeking something more to cling to, but this is it, the sky: their signal to blossom and set seeds. Halfway down, she spots some tight-furled buds.

For weeks she's watered without really looking, immersed in work: upgrading her website, selling at two vintage fashion and linens shows, and helping the heirs sort through the tight-packed storage units of an older dealer, a friend who'd been felled by a series of strokes. Sharon tells herself to slow down and appreciate today. Her bag over her shoulder, her amber beads rattling, she strides along Belle Meade's sidewalks, nodding at neighbors walking dogs she hopes won't all be pissing on her trellis.

At Biscayne Boulevard, she turns south. People are brunching outside at a hip eatery that's opened in a formerly run-down motel. When she was a child, the motels here were a tourist draw, but then came decline, prostitution, drugs, and crime that drove fearful homeowners out of the surrounding neighborhoods. Many of them really more alarmed, Sharon thinks, at hearing Spanish and Creole, and good riddance to them. New people, risk-takers, fond of Deco buildings and a bargain, bought in. With those who'd stayed, they formed a tribe of the resilient, pushing for police enforcement and rescuing past beauty. She's loved being part of this revival. She likes, more than anything, reuse. Make-do, the Victorians called it: repairing, repurposing.

Right here, on Biscayne, one afternoon ten years ago she came upon a parked truck piled high with rustic furniture, new-made, still smelling green. A pair of sun-leathered men from Georgia had loaded up and driven down to Miami where cash flowed faster. She bought a bent willow chair that she'd sat outside in hundreds of evenings in the unbuggy season. Last fall, finding the legs had disintegrated, she salvaged the high curved back and spokes, staked it up, laced it all with wire into a trellis, and planted seeds. What did the Victorian language of flowers call morning glory? She'll have to look it up. Wonderfully, the world now provides instant access to any public knowledge. Private knowledge, the way the chairs smelled, the truck and the men and that day's sense of opportunity, she doesn't forget.

*10:05 AM*

She has time before her hair appointment to stop by Stefan's shop. Last week he bought a few pieces she hadn't sold at the shows. He's at the counter with a customer, a man with wide shoulders, dark hair. She browses along a rack of jackets until she's close enough to view the man's profile. Handsome, but his mouth is tight. Perhaps his snakeskin cowboy boots pinch. A bit of a brute, but attractive. Young people would never believe that a woman deep into middle age observes lustfully, but appraisal at a glance is strong in her, as much for a man as a mantilla. He has a canvas bag spread open, showing a camera case. Not vintage.

Out of the changing stall pops a young woman, her dark hair in a long braid, wearing the piano shawl dress Sharon brought in last week. In 1910 it was a grand square of ivory silk, embroidered with fantastical red and blue flowers, bordered in long knotted fringe. Decades later, someone folded it on the diagonal, opened a simple neckline, cut into the sides to form sleeves, and seamed it with silk thread. It would look blowsy on anyone not young and slim, but for this girl, the dress flashes and slithers. The points front and back drip fringe to the tops of her strappy black shoes.

The man reaches and reads the price tag hanging at her wrist. She looks at him—appealing? demanding?—but he shakes his head. They're selling, not buying, Sharon understands. She spots watches in the man's bag. Possibly stolen, nothing Stefan will take. He wants men's cravats, vintage Oxfords, and shaving mirrors. Maybe he'll refer them elsewhere. The girl turns back into the dressing room, pulling off the dress. Sharon catches Stefan's eye and gives a moving-along-now wave.

*11:50 AM*

Sharon has savored every second of chat, color, shampoo, cut, and blow-dry. She feels fortified—not young, but groomed. Her hair, refreshed to her signature cherry-brown, is sleek. This shouldn't be wasted. Walking south, she texts Ray

Strout, her beau, as he likes to call himself, to ask if he wants to meet for lunch.

She reaches the Saturday Upper Eastside Farmer's Market booths clustered at the entrance to Legion Park. Pretty lettuce will just wilt if she carries it around. She buys a jar of honey, and, turning, recognizes the girl, now wearing a white top and skinny jeans, at a stand that sells drinks blended from fresh fruit. There's the man in the snakeskin boots, by the papayas.

The seller, a man in a broad straw hat, gives the girl a strawberry-colored smoothie. No money changes hands. They know each other, Sharon assumes. The beat-up canvas bag, on the ground by the man's boots, looks empty. He must have cashed in what he had to sell, somewhere. Both men watch the girl pull pink liquid through a straw, her pretty lips—and then Sharon turns away, and starts back north, thinking about the man who taught her the brevity of a girl's power.

Peter Lawler. She still has his last name. She slept with him in college and was immediately bound by expectations: Marriage after graduation. Teaching high school history while he did his Ph.D. (She'd been interested in the Victorians; he liked American radicals.) Two children. (He was angrier after the second, their son.) Moving for his teaching job at a small college in Pennsylvania. In theory it was her turn to study, but there was no graduate program. She was a department secretary, her hours constructed around on-campus daycare.

Prof. Lawler needed to turn his dissertation into a publishable book. On weekends, after he'd yelled about his need for quiet so he could *for once* concentrate, he typed and then went out to watch sports. Till one day, emptying his wastebasket, she saw, among crumpled pages, a draft of a love letter. Crouched, reading it, she found she wasn't surprised. Marriages made before the full flowering of availability were crashing all around them. She would have liked to fuck someone else, too, if she'd had the chance.

She remembers how, when she stood up, it occurred to her he'd left the letter on purpose, wanting her to blow up. So she didn't. She assembled evidence, bargained to go back to Miami with the children, and took a lump sum settlement—the next wife was a rich girl. Perhaps it was wrong not to tell the school he slept with students, but they denied him tenure anyway.

At their daughter's wedding, Dr. Peter Lawler, an administrator at a charter school in Tampa, was a balding stranger with a third wife. Still, Sharon remembers the width of his shoulders in his sweaty dorm cot, when she was 19, and how he praised her chestnut hair and high pointy breasts.

Who'd believe those breasts would become so plump and difficult to harness? Fortunately, she'd had some discreet fun, while raising the kids and living with her parents. And more fun, later, though she cherished her independence. There was a dull spell after she hit menopause, but then Ray, an antiques dealer just a few years older, took an interest. What does it matter that the silk shawl-dress would look silly on her? She does yoga and can walk miles without getting winded. She and Ray have been involved for a while, but decided to keep separate houses (his, a mess, hers orderly) and enjoy what they have without marrying. Or that's what she asked for, and he agreed. And now, he's texted her to say, "Sure! Meet U @ new restaurant." She uses the phone to learn that in the Victorian language of flowers the morning glory stands for Love in Vain. She assumes it's because each flower blooms one morning and shrivels by sunset. Yes, damn that Peter Lawler.

*12:45 PM*

She and Ray saw the new restaurant mentioned, last week, in a *New Times* piece on things to do in the "hot" Upper Eastside. Along the train tracks that form the western edge of the neighborhood, repainted warehouses now draw back their high metal gates on weekends to reveal decorator collections and art galleries. Reaching the address, Sharon finds bougainvillea framing an inner gate, a paved courtyard, artists' working studios, and the tiny bistro. Sharon chooses a courtyard table and reads the menu till Ray arrives. They order salads and the Spanish house white.

Their wine comes fast. They touch glasses. A former cop turned dealer in books and paper ephemera, Ray combines cheerful cynicism and a good heart. He describes today's estate sale, where he found old sheet music at a house on Biscayne Bay. "The side facing the water is all glass. Apparently, after the husband died," Ray says, "the widow left the piano untouched and never drew the curtains. Over time, the direct sun warped the instrument to unplayability. Sad waste of a baby grand."

No sooner does she think of the piano shawl dress than she sees the girl, wearing it, her hair loose over her shoulders. The man's hand is on her back as they cross the courtyard and sit at the bar, just inside the wide doorway. The man orders red wine with a snap of his fingers. She got him to buy the dress, Sharon thinks, and now he's angry.

"Like that outfit?" Ray asks.

"I sold the dress to Stefan. I saw these two, there, this morning. The guy was trying to sell some things that were—"

"Stolen?"

"Well, too new. Stefan wasn't buying." The canvas bag hangs from the back of the man's high seat at the bar. Sharon imagines the girl's jeans and top rolled up inside.

"She looks too young to get served," Ray whispers.

Sharon tries not to stare into the bar. Stefan's shop, the farmer's market, the bistro: the girl read the *New Times* piece and wanted a great day out, she thinks. And persuaded him it would work for whatever he was after.

The man has downed his wine. The girl frowns, then rushes hers. He drops money on the bar, stands, and grabs his bag. The girl steps down and pauses, smoothing her dress, and catches Sharon's eye. *Let him go*, Sharon thinks. The girl tosses her hair back and follows him.

Ray asks, "What is it, honey?"

She hushes him. As the girl strides by, the ripples in her hair catch sunlight. The silk fringes dance. What will become of her? Who is stronger? Sharon knows she'll never find out. This is just one of those glimpses you get, one moment in the city's unknown epic of desire and aspiration and loss.

Ray says, "Pretty dress. You should have kept it to wear."

"I'd look ridiculous."

"You only think so. And it would *feel* good." He runs his hand along hers.

She casts a glance at him. He's a cute man, with curly dark gray hair. She should appreciate him more. They linger over their salads, have more wine, then order espresso and split a piece of chocolate cake, the day is just so fine.

They stroll to her gate—it is, somehow, after four already. The morning glories have progressed. She shows him the long buds, their spirals now showing purple at the tips.

"Will they open tomorrow?"

"We'll have to see in the morning," she says, and leads him inside, and lets herself feel how it is to be a beloved old thing.

# RUINS
Susanna Daniel
*Stiltsville*

After we'd been waiting an hour for Charlie to arrive at the stilt house, my mother's boyfriend, Henry, and our neighbor, Mr. Calloway, started playing chess on a dusty set they'd found in a closet. Henry blundered his opening gambit and I pretended not to notice. I was almost fifteen, and the last time I'd been to Stiltsville had been more than a decade earlier. My memories of the place, of the summer my mother and I spent there with Charlie when I was four years old, were hazy flashes that dissolved when I tried to bring them into focus.

My mother and her friend Marse were there, too. Marse had barely known Charlie, but still she'd taken the day off to drive us across the bay in her little fishing boat. As soon as my mother and I had arrived at the marina, Marse had started bossing me. She told me to get the cooler from her SUV and fill it with ice. She pulled me into the boat and told me to count the life jackets, then sent me to the bow to untie the spring line and push us off. I had no time to think about all the water, which I suppose had been Marse's plan from the start.

As we cleared the marina, the Coast Guard trawled by, trailing a half-sunk sailboat. The grownups waved. Marse accelerated into the bay and the wind rose. I kept my eyes closed for a long time. I could feel my mother checking on me. "Look," she said, and when I did, I saw half a dozen structures hovering over the horizon. We were miles from shore. Did I remember this place, or only think I did?

Charlie was in town for a retrospective of his work. It would be professional suicide, Henry had said, for him to skip the opening. My mother had received a note with the date. The dinner that had never happened had been arranged, as well as this return to Stiltsville, this tour of ruins. It had been decided—by Charlie, I assumed—that he would come out with his accountant, a local, instead of with us.

This wasn't Charlie's old house. This house belonged to a friend of Marse's who'd loaned the keys. A few planks of the dock were rotting and a fire had burned out a section of the floor on the western porch. Before unlocking the gate and coming upstairs, we all stood on the open platform beneath the house and looked up at the underside of the second floor, where someone had used pink spray paint to scrawl: FREDDIE SUCKS DICK. My mother had covered her mouth. "This wasn't how it used to be," she said to me.

My mother went inside right away. I didn't follow her. I thought if I went inside, into the shuttered darkness and away from the water, I might never come out. I loitered in the doorway. She stood at the kitchen counter in her green sundress, slicing fruit. When she cooked at home, she hummed or sang, but today there was only the hard thump of the knife. There was also the wind and waves lapping the pilings, coming and coming. The clear, sun-bleached sky looked to me like white paint on white canvas.

I took a photograph in my mind of the way she looked as she worked, shoulders so alert. She caught me staring. "Shoo," she said, and turned back to the cutting board.

I found I was able to stand at the porch railing after I pressed my thighs against it to feel how it wouldn't give. The air was so hot that my own breath felt cool on my lips. Below, on the dock, Marse was struggling to thread line through a fishing pole. Her curses flared up like tiny fireworks; Henry and Mr. Calloway laughed. "I'll help," said Mr. Calloway, and went past me down the stairs.

Mr. Calloway didn't meet my eye anymore, and he didn't speak to me directly if he could avoid it. This was because of what had happened a year earlier, when I'd been at his house with his daughter Alyssa and her older sister Tanya, and some of Tanya's friends came over, and they all decided to play water polo in the Calloways' pool. I'd sat on the deck with my sketchpad. It was one of Tanya's friends who pushed Alyssa down, who swam away without noticing that Alyssa didn't come up. I was busy sketching one of the girls, who a minute earlier had bobbed straight out of the water like she'd been launched by a giant—but something tugged at me, and finally I looked up.

I hesitated, yes, but I did jump in. Tanya had seen it too, and she reached Alyssa first and pulled her out, and somehow I made it to the side of the pool without going under myself. After that day, when Alyssa came over, my mother went across the street first to get a ramp to cover our front steps. Alyssa told me—she still spoke, just a lot more slowly—that she thought she would walk again soon. I told her I agreed. Until a thing happens or doesn't, what's the difference between what we believe to be true, and what we want badly to be?

I think they all knew—Henry and Mr. Calloway and my mother and even Marse—that Charlie might not show. The night before, my mother had made me wear a button-down shirt and sit downstairs with her and Henry, who, it was obvious, had also been told what to wear. She'd made dinner and set the table in the dining room. The appointed hour came and went. We stopped trying to make conversation. After a while I looked up and my mother was standing at the window pressing the pads of her fingers into her eyelids. "Georgia," Henry said, and she said, "Please don't say anything."

Henry keeps a townhouse in Coconut Grove, though he's spent almost every night at our house for as long as I can remember.

She'd answered the phone when it rang. She turned away from us. She had not spoken to Charlie, on the phone or in person, in ten years, but still I thought I heard in her voice a kind of daily intimacy, like someone saying goodnight in a distracted way, knowing there would be a thousand more chances to do so.

My mother told me once that the human capacity for surprise is surprising in itself—the way we can know what's coming and still be astonished when it arrives.

When Mr. Calloway came back upstairs, Henry beckoned me over. "A little assistance, genius," he said, and with my help, Henry took Mr. Calloway's king's bishop pawn.

Back then, Charlie had lived at Stiltsville full-time. People called him the hermit. He didn't own a boat, and my mother had taken a summer job as his errand runner. Twice a week, in a boat she borrowed from her father, she spanned the miles between the shore and Stiltsville; she brought me with her. Soon, Charlie was teaching me to swim and fish and snorkel, and even to draw. Charlie's work was in galleries all over South Florida, and he gave me the wooden mannequin that still sits on the shelf behind my easel. As my mother put it, he was my teacher before I was even ready to learn.

When she talked about that summer, she blinked a lot and the corners of her mouth turned down. She spoke the way one speaks of something that started out wonderful and ended badly. This was the summer of Stiltsville and swimming and fishing; this was the summer of Charlie, who she loved. This was the summer she separated from my father. This, too, was the summer I fell head-first from Charlie's stilt house porch onto the dock, then into the water, and Charlie drove full-bore across the bay to Mercy Hospital while my mother held me and shouted at me to open my eyes. This was the last summer I swam, the last summer I walked without a limp, the last summer my left eye didn't wander a little when I was tired. This was the summer a hurricane destroyed Charlie's stilt house and six others, and Charlie left Florida, and us, for good.

We'd been waiting two hours. The chess game ended and Henry put away the set. Mr. Calloway came to stand beside me at the porch railing. He glanced over a few times before he spoke. "See there," he said, gesturing toward the watercolor skyline. "Freedom Tower. My father helped design it."

"Which one?"

He pointed again, but it was no use. We were so far away. "It looks small now, but back then it was the tallest building in Miami. I was raised here, like your mother. Like Charlie."

When my mother recalled the Miami of her childhood, she spoke of riding her bike to the soda fountain, of the Holsum Bakery that made the air smell like yeast, of ski shows in the bay, ladies in sequined bathing suits stacked in pyramids. The soda fountain was now a Walgreens. The bakery was a cineplex.

Mr. Calloway said, "I admire what you did today, coming out here."

I didn't know how to answer, so I nodded. My mother came out onto the porch carrying a rattan tray crowded with bowls of fruit and artichoke hearts, crackers and whitefish spread. Henry touched her back, but she turned away from him and tossed a cracker over the railing into the water.

"For the fish," she said. She looked calm, but her nostrils were wide and her voice pinched.

*Mom,* I wanted to say, *I got on a boat and crossed the water. I am standing here next to Alyssa's father, who hates me. I am wearing my own shame like the heaviest boots. It's pulling on me, but I'm standing here anyway, for you.*

My mother had told me again and again that no one blamed me. She'd said when a parent's child has an accident, that parent resents the whole healthy world. She'd felt the same after my accident, she said. She still felt it every time my friends went to the beach or my eye wandered or she caught me rubbing my leg.

Something snagged Marse's line and she gave a wallop. We all looked down at her. She panted and strained, mouth open in delight. My mother was holding my hand, though I didn't remember her taking it. I realized we weren't waiting for Charlie anymore, so much as we were waiting for time to pass, so we could go home.

The fish that burst out of the water glittered in the sunlight. My mother dropped my hand and ran down the stairs. Henry put an arm around my shoulders. At his house in Coconut Grove, he kept framed photographs and trinkets from travels and just-in-case winter sweaters. He'd been waiting for this day as long as my mother had.

The fish on Marse's line flapped as she worked to free it, and after a minute my mother took over, reaching with sure hands into the fish's mouth. I felt bad for the fish, but the air in my own lungs was coming deep and clean. Henry felt the same, I think, and maybe Mr. Calloway was feeling it, too. We watched the women and the wide green bay and the stilt houses in the distance—houses that, like the one beneath our feet, would be gone soon and forever, given over to vandals or fires or rot or hurricanes or some of each.

The words gathered in my throat. I almost said, *Charlie called back.* I almost said, *I was standing beside the phone when it rang, after you and Mom went upstairs. His voice was almost-but-not-quite familiar. He cleared his throat. He asked how I was. He told me he was proud of my painting, that I had enormous talent. He said he was very, very sorry.*

Marse and Mr. Calloway and Henry and my mother—I felt like I was at one end of a telescope and they were huddled together in my lens, making adulthood look overly complicated and long, but also very brave.

"He's not coming," I said to Henry.

"I know," Henry said.

My mother, kneeling on the dock, finally pulled out the hook. She dipped her hands in the water and the fish darted away. She didn't stand up. Marse stooped next to her, and my mother's body started to shake. I took a photograph in my mind. This is grief, I thought, but it's also freedom.

# IN PLAIN SIGHT
Corey Ginsberg
*North Bay Village*

By the time the waitress brought the plate of oysters, barnacled earlobes suspended in a quickly melting ice bed, Tate had whittled an inch off his second pitcher of Presidente. It was shaping up to be an afternoon of aggressive drinking.

Claire had left that morning. Not really left—the bitch gutted Tate's North Miami apartment. Rows of identical black shoes and their impossible heels, gone before he got up. Every bottle of lotion, hair spray, and hand sanitizer, yanked from the bathroom shelf. The only trace of what he referred to as their fourteen-month sleepover was the lone note she left on the kitchen counter, next to an empty box of her muesli cereal: *Fuck you, Tate.* Then, another note next to it, in bigger block letters on a stray piece of cardboard: *IN CASE YOU DIDN'T SEE THE LAST NOTE, FUCK YOU.*

Claire had also taken Rupert's bowl, leash, and that squeaky toy Tate got him for Christmas, the one that looked like a banana but sounded like a cancerous lung. She left the dog, though, as well as a puddle of piss Rupert dragged his epic

Basset Hound ears through. Tate stood in the piss while he read the note.

"Can I get you anything else?" the waitress finally asked. Tate didn't realize she'd been waiting there. Claire would have rolled her eyes at another example of his pathological obliviousness. He shook his head and forced a grin. All the servers wore blue tank tops and tiny black shorts. This one's forgettable face held taut with a standard ponytail. Tate watched her ass cheeks jiggle as she left with his first empty pitcher. It was the kind of ass that couldn't decide where the cheeks ended and the legs started. He'd tip her well.

Since he arrived at Shuckers Bar & Grill an hour earlier, Tate had stopped drinking only to scratch the colony of no-see-um bites erupting on his shins below his dress pants and to blot sweat from his forehead with a balled-up napkin. His phone vibrated again, a shuttering dance across the sun-slapped surface of the plastic table. Eight missed calls and three unchecked voicemails meant Tate was in deep shit. He had to tell Barry about the hearse.

Tate sat with his back to Biscayne Bay, a tough position to maneuver given the bar was practically straddling the water. He hated the ocean: its audacious consistency, mismatched with its unpredictability. And its smell—the salt sting followed by the sulfurous rot that demanded one's whole-nose focus. Waves slapped against the wooden barrier that separated land from water as he massaged the lump forming on his forehead. It wasn't bad enough to warrant medical attention, but provided him with a sufficient *wom-wom* headache to remind him just how screwed he was.

The first oyster went down smoothly, a lemon-infused, cold glob. The aftertaste, though, was less settling. In the back of Tate's mind was Mr. O'Rourke's thick, dead tongue—which he imagined was another substantial glob—in the rear of the hot hearse. Tate downed his glass of beer and pushed his index finger though the pitcher's expanding sweat halo.

July in Miami was annual punishment for living in a city with mild winters. The sun was a flaming middle finger. Tate wished he was sitting at one of the tables closer to the bar, beneath the yellow awning. He wanted to be like the other handful of customers, who were absorbed in the Yankees game playing on the nearest flat-screen. Instead, he let the sun beat down its appropriate punishment as he dialed his boss.

"Where the fuck are you?" Barry's voice was a guttural nightmare of chain smoking and decades of screaming at Heat games.

There was no good way to put it, so Tate didn't try. "I totaled the hearse, Barry." He sipped beer from the side of his mouth to mute the swallow, a move he'd learned early on while Claire was traveling and made her token 11 PM check-in calls.

"Shit. No you didn't. How bad?"

"Put it this way," Tate said as he watched the woman at the next table cut her son's grilled cheese into greasy wedges, then dump a mound of Heinz ketchup on top. "It's a good thing Mr. O'Rourke's already dead."

"Goddamn you, Tate. That Cadillac cost me seventy grand." Barry stopped long enough, Tate imagined, to take a bump from the lid of his Cross Pen, a move Tate had pretended to ignore dozens of times between viewings at the Tranquility Funeral Home. "We got four dozen AARP members on their way to the cemetery. I don't care if you have to drag the casket ten miles, you get that stiff there."

Tate poured another beer.

Here were the parts of the story Tate had left out: how the hearse was a good mile away on the John F. Kennedy Causeway, with some hippie car stuck in its back end. How he'd exchanged insurance information with the mouse of a lady who had plowed into him, who hadn't stopped screaming frantic Spanish into her cell phone long enough to realize Tate was leaving the scene. At first, just far enough from the crash to straighten out his aching head. Then, when she didn't wave him down or so much as notice his wandering, he let his legs keep going. Farther and farther away.

As Barry continued with his tirade, something in the corner of Tate's vision snagged his attention. A slow-moving mass in the water, not even fifty yards away. A manatee, maybe. Somehow he'd managed to live here for fifteen years and hadn't seen a single one. Claire had often pointed out there were entire worlds of things he overlooked.

"Tate, you there?"

An old man stood on the edge of the water with a hand cupped around his eyes, squinting into the bay. Hadn't he seen a manatee before? A few others gathered. Goddamn it, they lived in Miami. Hadn't they seen it all?

"Tate!" Barry shouted, then sniffled.

In their heated exchange last night, Claire had called Tate many things. Names he wished to drink from the conveyer belt of his memory and package in his warehouse of avoidance. But not her final gesture. Tate would never forget the image of Claire standing in the doorframe that separated the living room from the hall, her hands augmenting what he realized was a perfect protrusion on her normally flat stomach. "A second-trimester bulge, you prick," she said. Then she locked herself in the guest room for the night and cried waves of soft sobs. No amount of knocking or apologizing had been enough.

When he got up for work, Claire was gone.

Only Tate *did* notice things. He had tried, unsuccessfully, to remind Claire through the shut door that apparently they just weren't always the right things. He could see through people's bullshit. Didn't that count for something? He saw directly through his own bullshit, too. Like the routine that had punctuated every damn day of Tate's twenties and spilled over into his hideous thirties. He was practically a spectator at the absurd pittance of his life, playing like a scratched DVD that skipped over the best scene each time.

But he would do better. This was a promise Tate made to himself right before the car crash. He'd do better because he had to. Tomorrow, he'd do better than today. And so on—like an installation art exhibit of improving life moments. He would become a noticer of everyone and everything. Maybe then Claire would give him another chance.

Tate focused on the water. He realized that whatever was getting closer to the pier wasn't a fish at all—it was a person. Swimming. Thrashing. Heading this way.

"I gotta go," Tate said. He hung up before Barry could offer any more frenzied threats.

"What's that, Mummy?" the kid at the next table asked. He pointed a ketchup-stained finger at the bay.

"Just a fish, Sweetie," she said, barely glancing over.

The form was close enough for Tate to see every violent elbow lift and scissor kick. Other patrons gestured from their tables toward the water. Where had the swimmer come from? The closest land across the bay was miles from Shuckers, and the nearest boat, a yacht of some sort, bobbed in the distance, halfway to downtown.

Tate turned in his chair to get a better look. "That's not a fish," he said. "That's a naked woman."

He stood as she approached the dock. The woman took a few more sloppy strokes, then latched on to the closest of the fat wooden poles. The rest of them stood there, stupidly watching, as she began to shimmy her way out of the water. They gawked at her pale, flexed thighs and took in the insanity of her nakedness. The woman somehow managed to pull herself up the pole and flop facedown onto the deck. She was bone thin; her spine protruded with each breath as her naked body announced its exhaustion. Finally, the woman sat up and coughed.

What had begun as detached interest in the scene quickly escalated into gut-throbbing compulsion for Tate. She looked nothing like Claire. She was horrifying. Beautiful. Impossible.

The woman pulled what looked like a jellyfish off one of her breasts and threw it back in the water. Red splotches and small cuts adorned her stomach and arms. The mom at the next table gasped and covered her son's eyes just as the woman tossed her wild flame of long blonde hair behind her head.

Was this really happening? Sure, he was drunk, but Tate couldn't fathom a quantity of shitty beer that would make him hallucinate a naked woman. Especially one this good looking.

The woman climbed to her feet, flecks of the deck caught on her red kneecaps. Instead of speaking, she vomited a clear stream of what appeared to be ocean water and bile. She took a reluctant step forward, then another, as her body acclimated to land.

As she slowly staggered, the woman seemed to gain strength and confidence. Once she reached the stairs, her walk transformed into a lopsided jog. She didn't notice—or care—that dozens of eyes implored her as she plowed into the seating area and darted past the bar.

Where was this woman going? Was she running from, or toward?

Tate had to find out.

He reached into the pocket of his dress pants and retrieved a wad of cash. As the woman maneuvered around bar stools and made her way to the exit, Tate shoved the bills under the edge of the empty pitcher. Before he could understand his own forward momentum, his legs carried him away from the table. Tate nearly tripped over an unoccupied green plastic chair as he kicked off his dress shoes and undid his belt.

When he reached the parking lot, Tate peeled off his dress shirt and work pants. His undershirt tore when he pulled it from his chest. He hurried to catch up as the woman made a sharp left onto the 79th Street Causeway, barreling down the sidewalk along the busy street. Cars honked and swerved. Tate was down to his boxer shorts and white tube socks as he approached her.

As he ran, the telescope lens through which Tate had been looking at his life sharpened its focus. Everything grew clear as he zoomed in. He took off his boxers, then his socks.

"Wait for me—please!" he screamed to the woman as cars whizzed past. Tate wondered, with each huff and pant, just how far his legs would carry him.

*15 Views of Miami*

# MY PEOPLE
Geoffrey Philp
*Ives Dairy*

Steeling my nerves, I'd just lit a spliff and opened my third bottle of Red Stripe when my nosebleed began. Placing the spliff on the ashtray in the middle of the loveseat I used to share with Dorothy, my wife, I leaned back and stuffed a tissue in my nose.

As I gazed up at the ceiling fan, I wondered why the nosebleeds had become so frequent. Before Dorothy died nine days ago, I never got nosebleeds. But now, it's every evening when I come home to this empty house, wondering what I'm going to microwave for dinner.

Back in Jamaica, even if you had been an only child and both your parents died, this would never have happened. For nine nights of mourning, family and friends would have been visiting with food and drink. But in America, you live alone and you die alone.

Dust had gathered on the edge of the fan blades. Dorothy had asked me to clean them, but I'd been distracted. Chalk it up to one more chore I needed to do since we'd brought this house back from the dead.

The bleeding stopped, so I leaned forward. My head felt like a swollen pumpkin. The room was suddenly cold. When I looked up, a white man was sitting on the sofa in front of me. The hairs on my arm stood on end.

"Hell hath no fury like a woman scorned," he said, and crossed his legs. I almost jumped out of the chair.

"Who are you? How did you get in here?"

"Name's Bill Falkner. I'm the original owner——"

"But I thought——"

"Yes, I'm dead. Suicide. I'm stuck here."

I felt like running, but I couldn't. When you come from Jamaica, duppies are a serious matter. I thought I was hallucinating. Carlton, my herbsman, must have laced my weed. But Carlton would never do that. He's been growing the best weed in Miami for as long as I've known him.

"You still haven't answered my question," I said, reverting to my best attorney's tone.

"I don't know how I've been able to do this. Since you and your wife moved in, I've amused myself by slamming doors and windows."

"That was you?"

"And the occasional brushing up against your wife. It was enough to scare away the other owners, but you stayed. Why?"

"I've put too much work into this house and I know a good bargain when I see one."

"My mother said the same thing when she bought it back in 1958. What year is it now?"

"Twenty-thriteen. You don't know?"

"You can't measure eternity. I've gauged the passing of time by the people who've lived here. You're the second black family to move in, so I imagine the times have changed. How are things for your people?"

*My people.* From some reason, that phrase bothered me. I still couldn't believe what was happening. What would my clients think? I, the most business minded and the only confirmed atheist in my firm, was having a conversation with a ghost?

"Excuse me," I said, and got up from the loveseat. Now I understood why the house, a four-bedroom, two-bath with a pool for only a hundred thousand, had been on the market for so long. Cynthia, our real estate agent had mentioned supernatural events in the house, which scared Dorothy. I dismissed it as female hysteria. I guess I was now a believer.

I walked over to the kitchen sink and filled a glass of water. The phrase had stuck with me. Who were *my people*? Were they Jamaicans who had been leaving the island since our unofficial civil war? My Haitian brothers who were still fleeing after the earthquake? My African American brothers who were now celebrating Black History Month?

I finished the glass of water and walked back over to the loveseat. I put out the spliff and sipped the Red Stripe, which was now warm. Hot or cold, Red Stripe is better than insipid Miller.

"What do you mean by my people?"

"You know exactly what I mean," he said. "It's why your wife killed herself."

"How did you——"

"You were the one fucking your client upstairs when she caught you."

"The police said it was an accident."

"And you, a black lawyer, believe everything the police tell you?"

"But why?"

"You know why."

Did he know everything? I wanted to light the spliff, but I didn't. I tried to turn on the television, but it didn't work. Nothing electrical worked and soon it would be night.

My nosebleed started again. Dorothy knew I was gay from the first time she tried to kiss me. Even after I told her, she still agreed to get married after we graduated from law school. We also made a deal that we'd never have children. She may have been in love with me, but I wasn't in love with her. It was strictly a business arrangement. Dorothy allowed me to have my affairs as long as I was discreet and maintained our image in the community.

And it's not like I was going to come out. No Jamaican, no matter how desperate he was, would hire a battyman lawyer. They would rather go to a straight lawyer, no matter how incompetent he was.

Besides, Dorothy had gotten what she wanted. We were a famous power couple fighting for the rights of our people. We were photographed at every charity event, meet-up, and fundraiser, congressional and presidential, in Miami. We even had a picture with President Obama.

I closed my eyes, squeezed my nose and leaned back again for about a minute. When I released my hold, Bill was still there.

"I'd love to stay and chat, but I gotta go."

"I hope he was worth it," he said. "Sometimes life gives us exactly what we want, but there's always a hidden price."

"Try not to be here when I get back." I slipped on my jacket that I'd left hanging on the back of the loveseat and picked up my keys. "Why did you kill yourself?"

"I contracted AIDS. But it's not what you're thinking. Got it from a dancer in a titty bar up in Davie. I was wasting away in the house, so I said fuck it!"

Bill faded into the sofa when I turned on the outside lights. I turned on the alarm, which I'd forgotten to do when my wife found me in our bed with Stephen.

As I walked down the driveway toward my car, I glanced at my garden. The starburst bush I'd rescued from the city dump was now in full bloom. I marked time by the dying and flowering of plants in my yard.

Slipping on my seatbelt, I turned on the ignition. I don't like to wear seatbelts, but I was going over to Aventura, where the cops pull you over for driving while black.

Traffic, as usual, was a nightmare on Ives Dairy Road. I glanced over at the open area where they usually held bluegrass concerts. My next-door neighbor, Miguel Rojas, told me they used to hold KKK rallies there until white flight made it possible for our people to move into the neighborhood.

Despite the traffic jams, one of the advantages of living in Ives Dairy is that in a few minutes you're in the heart of Aventura, where people are always jogging. I guess when you're that rich, you can afford to jog and live off the interest in your portfolio or trust fund.

Although they owned their own ad agency, Stephen and his wife had neither, which is why they were underwater and needed my help. Since the recession, their company's revenues had been falling steadily.

From the moment Stephen stepped into my office, I knew his secret. It's always in the eyes. You can always tell a man who's sucked wood. I was determined to make that brown man choke.

And that he was married, like me, would insure secrecy. I used every delaying tactic I knew, not only with the mortgage company, but also with Stephen so I would see him regularly.

Still it came with a price. When I brought them to the brink of foreclosure, I made my move. I told Stephen that I'd do the rest of the filings *pro bono*, but I needed assurances.

Stephen knew exactly what I meant.

The first time we had sex, it was in my office and it went exactly as planned. I had that brown boy squealing with pleasure. I may be gay, but I'm a pitcher, not a catcher.

The more I got to know Stephen, I was amazed how our lives had crisscrossed in Jamaica and Miami. When we were younger, we did everything to appear normal———hanging out with the guys, smoking, and playing dominoes. But our fathers knew we were gay and disowned us. Still, he had it easier. He was brown and I was black. For every success that we shared———first in our family to go to college, graduating at the top of our class———he had skated by on his middle-class charm and I had to claw my way up.

By the time Stephen and his wife were back on track with their mortgage payments, I'd fallen in love with him. And not just because he had a body that was sculpted like Usain Bolt's, but because Stephen was also an idealist——— trying to right every wrong in this world. This week, the exoneration of Marcus Garvey, the next week orphaned kids of mothers with AIDS.

"If I ever had a kid, I'd never want him to go through what I went through," he said.

"Like that's ever gonna happen," I said as I held his shoulders to my chest.

And that was how Dorothy caught us. Me whispering in Stephen's ear. I'll never forget the look on his face when she left.

But now she was dead. I didn't have to live a lie anymore. And neither did Stephen. With the insurance settlement that I'd received, we could move to Washington, get married and smoke all the medical marijuana we wanted. We'd be free.

I parked in his driveway and rang the doorbell.

Slowly, he opened the door. "What are you doing here?"

"I thought we could talk. You wouldn't return my calls, so I came over."

"Who is it, dear?" asked his wife. She wore a t-shirt that said "Stop Keystone" and cradled a baby in her arms.

"It's Ronald, our lawyer. He stopped by to see how things are going."

"Why don't you come in, Mr. Williams. Stephen and I would like to thank you for all you've done for us."

"No, he was just leaving, dear. Doctor's visit."

"Well, thank you, Mr. Williams," she said. "Drop by any time."

"Why didn't you tell me," I squeezed the words through my teeth.

"The adoption was finalized last week. His mother died from AIDS. It's the least we could do for the cause."

"I thought we——"

"There was never any we," he said and closed the door in my face.

On the drive home, I stopped near the canal where the police found Dorothy's car. Over at the middle school, a soccer game was in full swing. I used to play soccer in high school. Me and my teammates almost beat our goalie to death because we suspected he was gay. His father took him out of the school and, a few years later, they moved to Miami. I saw him one night on South Beach, cruising the gay bars. I was so envious.

As I pulled into my driveway, the lights flickered. I opened the door and checked the alarm. Ever since the financial crisis and with so many people out of work, our safe neighborhood had become a bit more dangerous.

I closed the door behind me. At least, I was back in the sanctuary of my home. I tried to turn on the lights, but they didn't work. The smell of Dorothy's perfume filled the house.

Out of the darkness, I heard Bill's voice.

"I've finally figured it out. I'm leaving here. Your wife is coming back here and she's mad as hell."

"What should I do?"

"Run," he said. "Run!"

# NOT WITHOUT FEATHERS

Leonard Nash
*Key Biscayne*

I was subbing for a calculus teacher at MAST Academy when Monica Feathers appeared on Career Day to speak about stocks, bonds, mutual funds, and exchange-traded derivatives to this group of smarty-pants eleventh graders. I asked for her card and called her that night. We chatted awhile and planned a date for Sunday afternoon, across the Rickenbacker Causeway on Hobie Beach.

I'll be honest with you—her name bothered me. Monica Feathers sounds like a character in a straight-to-Netflix mumblecore flick about over-caffeinated postgraduate poetry students in Greenwich Village. But she was an investment advisor, worked for an outfit with offices in New York, San Francisco, and Brickell Avenue.

Besides substitute teaching, I was writing my first novel, about an Amway executive who scams everyone from Jeb Bush to Rick Sanchez, buys the Miami Dolphins, moves the team to Anaheim, pays everyone off courtesy of a California Public Improvement Bond, and hosts a new syndicated show called *Ponzi Apprentice, Los Angeles*. This was not autobiographical. I drove a salvage-title Honda bought from a jai-alai player in Dania Beach, and my wardrobe came from thrift stores and Ross Dress for Less.

Before the date, I researched Monica Feathers. She owned a two-bedroom oceanfront condo a mile south of the Tennis Center. Fair is fair. I'm sure she did some recon on me. She and her ex-husband, a pro golfer no one's ever heard of—Carlton Murphy—paid $775,000 at the peak of the market. Now it appraised for $580,000. I was renting a one-bedroom atrocity in Kings Creek that I found on Craigslist for $935 a month.

Monica Feathers arrived in denim shorts, cotton t-shirt, leather flip-flops, and Ray-Bans. From our spot in the scarce shade of a young coconut tree, I could see the Seaquarium's geodesic dome.

"It's big," I said, pointing at the Escalade she'd parked beside my 2002 Accord.

"I was leasing a Beetle convertible, but I'm always taking clients to lunch and driving them to the airport. I hate it, but in my business, it's all about appearances."

"I don't care what my stockbroker drives," I said, quoting something I'd read in the *Herald*. "I want to know what his clients drive."

"We're a boutique wealth management firm for high-income clientele—celebrities, mostly athletes, but you'd be surprised what some *regular people* are worth. I've got a retired mailman in the Northeast with a million-dollar portfolio. So what *does* your stockbroker drive?"

"You kidding? I've got a checking account at Wells Fargo, whatever cash is in my wallet, and that nifty four-door with the dented quarter panels."

"I was hoping your Lamborghini was in the shop," Monica Feathers said with a half-smile. "Look, it's fine… it's refreshing, actually." Monica Feathers pulled sunblock from her bag, rubbed the white cream on her smooth legs. She slipped off her t-shirt, revealing a simple black bikini top. "Here," she said. She turned her back to me and sat there in some cross-legged yoga pose on my U-Haul moving blanket.

"My folks brought me out here when I was little," I said, rubbing SPF 50 on her shoulders and back. "My dad would park his Oldsmobile right on the beach, between the Australian pines Hurricane Andrew wiped out. In high school, we called the Key Biscayne kids 'Key Rats,' always blabbering about whose dad owned a bigger boat and who skied in Utah over spring break."

"Now they're fat and bald and popping ED pills," Monica Feathers said. "Thanks, that's good." She reached for the lotion tube.

Despite our mismatched tax brackets, we got involved. The sex was phenomenal. Okay, maybe not phenomenal, but great. Above average, for sure. That is, when she had time for me. Weekdays, Monica Feathers worked ten-hour days and spent most evenings entertaining clients at fancy restaurants and hotel bars from Coral Gables to South Beach. On a good day, her refrigerator might contain a re-corked bottle of Fat Bastard pinot noir, a six-pack of Red Stripe, a tub of spreadable butter, sliced pumpernickel, and one onion.

Meantime, I might be subbing for the journalism teacher at Gables High, a PE coach at Palmetto Middle, an English teacher at Braddock. Besides the stash of dry-erase markers and hall passes, you'd be surprised what teachers leave in their desks—cigarettes, pay stubs, Xanax, dog-eared copies of *Fifty Shades of Grey*.

Meanwhile, I was plugging away on my novel, drafting scenes in the teachers' lounge during planning periods. And without any pets or plants, I was mobile. Early on, Monica Feathers took me on some of her weekend trips—New Orleans; Baltimore; Kingston, Jamaica; even Providence, Rhode Island for her high school reunion. She carried an Amex Black Card. Before Monica Feathers, I'd never heard of those, but I liked the sound of it—damned thing's made of platinum—so I gave one to my novel's protagonist. He bought a 2014 Corvette Stingray with it. Awesome car, but in revision, I changed it to a Ferrari F12 Berlinetta. *What the hell? It's not my money. It's not even his money.*

Friday afternoons, when Monica Feathers was in town, I'd shoot over to Key Biscayne, grab takeout from China Garden on Crandon Boulevard, or pop into Winn Dixie for fresh tilapia or a roasted chicken. I'd bring DVDs from the public library. We had a thing for John Hughes and Quentin Tarantino movies. Some nights, we'd sit on her balcony, which was larger than my living room, looking out at the ocean, sipping wine and playing music on her iPad. We made a game of seeing how long we could carry on a conversation comprised of nothing but song titles and lyrics. We'd take turns suggesting the artist— The Smiths, The Cranberries, Counting Crows, Simon and Garfunkel. Couple times we made love out there and spent the night cuddled in a sleeping bag.

\*

About seven months along, she was taking the weekend trips without me, said she needed to focus on work, meet certain quotas if she was ever going to make partner. That fall, we went a month without getting together. Weekend after weekend, she was away—golf clients in California, ballplayers in Chicago, some banking conference in Toronto. I completed additional paperwork for the Department of Education, watched movies on basic cable, worked out in the Kings Creek gym, and hung out at the pool editing my novel.

Monica Feathers texted me on a Wednesday afternoon, said we needed to talk. I suggested the former zoo, now called Gardens of Crandon Park. Close as it was to her place, we'd never been there together, nor could I remember seeing her on a Wednesday.

I arrived early, strolled around the refurbished carousel—I've got faded Polaroids somewhere, me and my cousins riding that thing when we were about five—then waited on a bench as geese, peacocks, and peahens meandered by. Monica Feathers arrived in one of her *Dry Clean Only* pantsuits and pulling *my* suitcase.

"I think this is everything," she said.

"Why?"

"I'm almost forty," she said.

"You're thirty-seven."

"My birthday was last week."

I said some things, Monica Feathers said some things, and then she quoted lyrics from a Cranberries song, about a girl ending things with her boyfriend, and how he'd be alone forever.

"Please don't plagiarize our breakup."

"This isn't going anywhere. *You're* not going anywhere, with your novel and your substitute teaching. In a way it's charming, but what's your plan? At least teach full-time. You have the certifications."

"I'm starting a memoir," I said. "My relationship with my parents was complicated."

"You can't live in the past," Monica Feathers said.

"It's the only place I know," I said.

"Last week I saw my ex-husband in Pebble Beach," she said near the former crocodile pond.

"I spent last week in Homestead, spoon-feeding puréed tuna sandwiches to profoundly retarded teenagers and helping change their diapers."

"Carlton's retiring," Monica Feathers said. "He missed the cut the last five tournaments, decided it's enough. He never really came back from his spleen surgery. Says he could see us having kids. That was always the primary issue."

"Did you sleep with him?"

"When you and I met, I wasn't looking."

"I wasn't either," I said, which was a lie. My suitcase wheels dragged some pebbles as we approached the former primate enclosure, now covered with painted manatee, deer, and pelicans, probably some local art-class project. Farther along, I pointed out the overgrown island where the elephants once roamed. The concrete benches looked unchanged from when the crowds departed for the new zoo in 1980.

"I have a photograph of my parents sitting there, my father with his wooden cane, my mother with a Stephen King paperback. Behind here was the hippopotamus enclosure." The wall was now encased in gnarled ficus roots. "By the way, I finished my novel last week," I said. "And I might have a lead on an agent. An English teacher I know is friends with a writing professor at FIU, and he's got a guy in New York. Or maybe Boston. Whatever, it's a lead." I could tell she wasn't impressed. "If that doesn't pan out, I'll give it another proofread and stick it up on Kindle. That's how everybody's publishing these days."

"You're writing a novel about a Ponzi schemer," Monica Feathers said, "but that's not who I am."

"I outlined the story long before we met, and either way, how would you know? I never showed you the manuscript."

"The Amex Black Card, it's called Centurion. You should fix that. You left a flash drive on my nightstand. I read the manuscript on the flight from San Francisco."

Before I could stop myself, I said, "I know what you paid for your condo, and I know what it's worth. Bet you've got as much equity as I've got in my crappy apartment."

"This was never a competition," Monica Feathers said. "But since you're so interested, I own my place outright—despite the equity loss—along with Penthouse #3, which I acquired when I foreclosed on the private loan. I bought two sixth-floor units from the bankrupt developer, and I own a townhouse off Ives Dairy Road. I think my new tenant was some sort of grand poobah in the KKK, but that's another story. My investment properties are all held under my corporate name, Not Without Feathers, LLC. You should have learned all this when you were snooping around on me."

"So you're loaded."

"Whatever I have is legit, and no, Carlton didn't pay for any of it. I supported him until the last year of our marriage when he finally won a tournament."

"You looked at my data drive. The stuff about your properties is public record."

"Here's what you don't know. Until I was twelve, we lived in a third-floor walkup near McCoy Stadium in Pawtucket. I used a lunch card all through school, and I took out student loans for college and my MBA. And the retired mailman whose tidy portfolio I manage—that's my dad. He busted his ass, trudging through rain, snow, sleet, hail, the whole kit and caboodle, so he could care for me and my brothers after Mom died."

We reached what had been the lion enclosure. Most of the corroded steel bars had been removed since the last time I was down there, maybe a year before. We sat on the rotted bench that once served as a perch for lethargic lions peering back at kids and parents strolling by with their popcorn and Instamatic cameras.

"So, since you read my novel, what did you think?"

"See my notes on the flash drive—it's in your suitcase—some ideas for the business shenanigans. It's a fun read."

An older black woman rolled by on her beach cruiser. She stopped, straddled the seat. "Oh my! You two look so cute sitting together in that cage. My name's Dorothy. May I take your picture?"

"Not a great time," I said.

"It's okay, Dorothy," Monica Feathers said, scooting closer to me. Her slacks snagged on the jagged wood. "Go ahead." Monica Feathers held my hand, leaned against my shoulder, our feet dangling from the edge of the lion bench. The orange and indigo sunset had settled behind the royal palms, casting long shadows across the lake.

"One more," the woman said, adjusting her fancy SLR, "this time with a flash. And you kids smile! It's a beautiful night!" She clicked several more photos, lowered her camera. "Have a blessed evening," she said, and peddled into the fading light.

"I guess this is it," I said, after the third loudspeaker warning that the park was closing. Our feet rested on my suitcase, barely visible in the near darkness. "They'll lock us in here."

"Wouldn't be the worst thing," she said. "I've got Clif Bars in my purse, and we can pee in the grass over there."

"Speaking of teaching full time, I filed my application with the district a few weeks ago." No doubt she saw the paperwork on my data drive. "As for us," I said, "we never discussed the future, figured you couldn't see one with me. We never got to the 'I love you' stuff."

"I'm still here," Monica Feathers said, "beside you in the dark."

"I don't know that one," I said. "*Please*, just talk to me."

"It's not a song," Monica Feathers said. "It's just me. And I'm still here."

# SINKHOLE
M.J. Fievre
*Little Haiti*

When the earth opened up and swallowed her husband Jonah whole, Pica feared that her life and all its private lies would be exposed. Reporters from the *Miami Herald* and the *Sun Sentinel* swarmed her mother-in-law's *botánica*, curious about the newly widowed Pica and the Little Haiti Man who'd been gulped down by the sinkhole. She tried to look devastated enough, but truth was she and Jonah had been sleeping in separate bedrooms for a while now. She'd considered leaving him, but her raven-haired Italian lover Bruno needed the money, and quite frankly Pica enjoyed being kept. Jonah had money in trust funds—lots of it—and Pica didn't want to go back to waitressing at Le Bébé, the Haitian diner. Jonah hadn't pushed for a divorce; he loved showing off his young and beautiful wife at banquets and fundraising galas, her body confident and tall, and she knew to hold him close in public and whisper in his ear as other investors drank martinis and referred to the neighborhood as Buena Vista, *not* Little Haiti, a name that brought images of dark-skinned boat people.

She'd spent that Thursday afternoon with Bruno while Jonah, recovering from allergies, took a nap in the claustrophobic, soon-to-sink master bedroom. Bruno and she drank Chianti and ate loaves of bread with imported French cheeses on the uneven wooden floor of his bare little flat behind the Little Haiti Cultural Center, read *The Miami Times*, fucked on his old pullout sofa under the big picture window, sunlight streaming in through the curtains, talked, and smoked *Comme Il Faut* cigarettes. They were a tangle of arms, legs, mouths, hands, and skin, and could not say where sex began and ended.

Pica felt womanly, testing the world for its possibilities. While Bruno pleasured her, she lost herself in his paintings, brilliant colors over dark tones, dashes of pure white paint, bright reds thickened with sand to build up textures.

\*

She'd returned home just in time to hear the deafening noise and find Jonah's room gone—his king-size bed, his mahogany dresser, his wide-screen TV. Pica jumped into the hole and frantically shoved away rubble with her bare hands, mapping in her mind the irises of Jonah's eyes, the palms of his hands, the sound of his voice. She didn't hear the police sirens; she didn't feel the landslide pinning her body parts. Although it was as if her body was sinking into flames, she didn't realize she was trapped waist-deep in rocks until a sheriff's deputy pulled her to safety, next to her mother-in-law, Philomena, a woman gone mad, hollering at the sky, blaming Pica, *la bruja*, for this tragedy. You don't want a baby—and the baby dies. You don't want my son—and the earth swallows him whole. Maybe Pica still smelled of sex. She'd wanted to shower, but in Bruno's apartment the water was brown no matter how long you ran it.

Something rumbled the next street over and Pica thought: *another sinkhole* while she waited for the ground to crack and crumble. But then there was the *beep-beep* of the truck backing up.

*

On Saturday, the rescue team gave up on looking for Jonah, and on Sunday a giant red backhoe gouged into the Little Haiti home as the neighbors watched, whispering in rushed Creole, everyone sluggish and greasy-looking in the heat rising off the engine in cellophane waves. Pica finally wept as a worker in an orange uniform and helmet handed her a family Bible that bore claw marks from the backhoe's bucket, along with a framed portrait of her husband. In the picture, taken only a few weeks before, Jonah was fit, in early middle age, with alert, hawkish features and a trim goatee. You could tell he was a man of immovable solidity. He had kept Pica from falling apart after she'd lost the baby, taking care of her with the kind of efficiency and calming confidence that made him what he was: solid granite.

By Monday afternoon, all the walls of the house were gone. Philomena reluctantly opened her doors to Pica, allowing her to take refuge in the back of the *botánica*, in Jonah's teenage bedroom, where the pillows were plumped, fluffed, and patted to prefigure sleep. A dull, dry ache had taken root in the back of Pica's head; she wanted to sleep but her eyes kept flipping open, and she looked out the windows at the backyard, overgrown and colorless as an old man's chest hair. She turned the TV volume down so low she couldn't hear anything but the mumbling of Philomena in the room next door. When Pica looked up, she saw a sinkhole pixilated on Channel 7.

A baby was crying somewhere, and Pica thought about the soft, lavender color they'd planned to paint their baby's room. She imagined the baby lying asleep on his bed, one fist clenched and raised over his head. Pica remembered her morning sickness; she once vomited on the sidewalk, drenching a colony of ants. Even though she hadn't wanted it, the baby inside her was so much a part of her, Pica often talked to it as she smoothed her blouse down over her slightly rounded belly.

Pica checked her cell phone for a text message, or any acknowledgement of her existence, from Bruno. She stared at her iPhone, touched the screen, tried to will messages to appear.

"I wanted to give you some time," Bruno said, when Pica finally showed up at his doorstep. His hair smelled like old cigarettes and pine. He was working on a painting of a couple waltzing inside a cage. Rich and glowing, the color harmonies captured the play of light and shadows and the sharp contours. The brush strokes blended harmoniously in warm yellow-gray, pink and green shades.

Leaning into the cushions, chewing a thumbnail, Pica focused her attention on the scar on the bottom of his chin where his skin was cut and the scab was prematurely picked. Then she rolled onto her back, corpse-like. "I couldn't get him out," she said. She curled her feet in toward each other and then pointed them straight down. "I tried so hard." Her voice was a shiver. "I wanted to tell him I was sorry about the baby. I'm haunted by his astonished look of hurt and disappointment when I told him I didn't want to keep it. Maybe he thought I did something to lose it." Pica rolled onto her side, pulled her knees up as much as she could stand and cried into her hand.

Bruno put down his paintbrush and went into the kitchen to make them each a rum and Coke. He handed her a glass and she sat up to gulp it down. He lay on his back and sipped his. "What are you talking about?"

She grabbed him by the chin, forcing him to look at her. "Bruno, don't you want us to be together?"

He steadied the drink on his chest. "We are together." He took up the glass and tipped an ice cube into his mouth and crunched it. "Fucking Jesus," he said. "You need time to grieve."

"Do you hear it?" Pica asked.

"What?"

"The baby. I hear it crying." She looked at him. "I have no idea whether it was going to be a boy or girl."

Bruno was pale. "There's no baby crying, Pica."

*

On her way back from Bruno's, Pica stopped by Simonise's apartment, not too far from the Libreri Mapou bookstore. There was an old cot with a broken leg propped up against the porch railing, and a rusty old grill with a layer of mummified charcoal from who knew when. Pica perfectly understood Jonah's need to find comfort in the bed of his Cuban mistress. After she'd lost the baby, she'd become cold and distant, toxic even. When she didn't withdraw completely, she screamed, banged doors shut, threw things. Until she met Bruno—someone who didn't know her too well, didn't know about the baby she'd lost months before the affair. She found herself again.

"Do you know about Jonah?" Pica asked as soon as the Havana woman opened the door.

Pretty but unmemorable, Simonise looked exhausted, a crying baby in her arms, maybe two weeks *pequeño*, wrapped in a yellow blanket like a little enchilada. "I heard about Jonah," she said.

*She is too tired for sadness,* Pica thought. The baby wouldn't stop crying. *Or maybe it's me.* She couldn't tell. The one thought was overwhelming: Her husband and child both somewhere without her, not breathing. The baby in Simonise's arms was still fussing, and Pica wanted to offer him her breast. She wanted him to feed on her, hungrily.

*

Bruno didn't answer his door and his cell phone went straight to voicemail. Pica tried to get a glimpse of him at every intersection, every street corner, every parking lot. On Friday and Saturday nights she looked for him at Churchill's Pub on Second Avenue. She attended art shows at the Little Haiti Cultural Center, hoping to see him appear in his beret, turtle neck, and faded jeans. At the Sunday Stroll, in front of the abandoned Methodist church transformed into a "funky" arts space for the occasion, she passed young couples with strollers, and she ran her hands over her stomach where her baby had been, and she cried on the inside at its slack flatness.

She didn't want to imagine some other woman spreading her legs as Bruno pushed himself into her wet body. She remembered her lover's cock—how it pulsed, stretching her. *Fuck you, Bruno Taravella! Eventually you'll be home*, Pica thought. There was a baseball bat sitting next to a chair in Philomena's garden. She grabbed it, then drove once again to Bruno's apartment on 59th Terrace. She would smash the bat into the side of his head, sending him face-first into the dirt.

She turned off the car's lights and waited in the dark—waited and waited—her hands trembling around the bat, until she finally spotted the pick-up truck around the corner—an old black thing with a Dave Matthews Band sticker on the back window. Maybe Pica would aim for the mouth—crack!—and Bruno would be spitting out blood and chunks of shit that he would only realize later to be his God-given teeth.

Pica used to believe in an all-encompassing love. She used to believe that love was a force, similar to a god, which was bigger than humans, bigger than loneliness and alienation. But, in reality, love always ended. Lovers had a glimpse of paradise, but humanity prevailed: mistakes were made, lives and loves were lost, and grief made the most bitter sort of loneliness.

As soon as he came out of the vehicle, Pica swung. The more Pica missed, the angrier she became, and then she started swinging even harder.

"Pica, stop," Bruno said, dodging, retreating behind an ylang-ylang tree, but she didn't want to hear.

She kept swinging, and swinging, and swinging.

Until she heard the baby crying again.

"Do you hear it?" Pica asked. "The baby?"

"There's no baby, Pica," Bruno said.

She put down the baseball bat, and Bruno didn't try to stop her as she started down the street, swallowed by the Miami shadows, invisible to the Little Haiti hookers, the unshaven men making drug deals beside a dumpster. She followed the baby's cries to her old street, to the place where the house Jonah had built her used to tower above palm trees and bougainvilleas and hibiscus trees.

A woman stood there, and she held a crying baby in her arms. It was Simonise.

"I'll never see Jonah again, will I?" Simonise said, looking at the hole in the ground, its perimeter surrounded by police tape.

*Nothing beats a sinkhole for swallowing a life*, Pica thought, to absorb the bitterness of loss and betrayal, the gallstones of desperation and deceit.

Simonise held the crying baby toward Pica and said, "I never wanted it." With her one free hand, she touched her belly. "I considered getting rid of it, you know. But Jonah begged me not to; he said he would bring his son home once you were ready."

Pica remained quiet, terrified.

Simonise frowned. Her jeans matched the gray pavement so her legs sort of melted into the road. "He's your responsibility now. It's either you or the firehouse."

Only when the baby stopped crying did Pica take him from his mother. He smiled.

"Good," Simonise said. "The doctor says he's normal, healthy. He cries a little and sleeps a lot." She looked Pica in the eyes. "Jonah loved him."

*

On her way back to her car, Pica sang to the baby, sang to the moon, her eyes unblinking in the dark that lay over her, thinking thoughts she wouldn't turn into words out loud, thoughts she would swallow whole and force into inexistence. Bruno's pick-up truck was gone from the driveway. She wouldn't worry about him. She was a mother now. A mother was warm and good, not cold and fearful. She sang to Baby Israel, and she sang to the moon, her heart pumping a passion that caused both pleasure and pain.

# WHAT COMES BEFORE THE GHOST
### J. David Gonzalez
*Allapattah*

t's a bright shimmering Wednesday and Carlos Zambo, twenty-six, police officer, pocked face and nothing resembling handsome, gets his first call of the morning. A break-in at Aves en Cuando on the northwest corner of 19th and 20th. It's a pet store. Specifically, birds.

Its address is like a million others in Allapattah. A crushed gravel parking lot smothered in cheap tar. A narrow strip mall, each business sitting shoulder to shoulder, each shop a slapdash emporium. Shipping companies and sneaker stores, boxing gyms and barbershops. The Aves en Cuando sits at the far end of the lot and has for neighbors a wig shop, a botanica, and an ice cream parlor. Along the wall, street kids painted an enormous parrot soaring over an inexact version of the Caribbean, the shop's name in graffiti letters above it.

Zambo backs into a space opposite the storefront. He steps out of the car and sees the shop's owner, Francisco De Luz, already ambling towards him. The old man wears a wife-beater ringed in sweat and smokes a cigarillo. His face is a wrinkled pooch.

"Finally," says De Luz. "What time is it? Seven? Seven-fifteen?"

"Six thirty."

"Good. I open at nine in the morning. And I want you to know that I plan to open at nine in the morning. I can't believe what they did to my store, but I can't worry about that now. You need to find them. And I need to open for business. You ready? I don't need someone wasting my time. Let's go." He grabs Zambo by the arm and leads him toward the store.

Zambo pulls his arm back, doesn't follow De Luz. "One second," says Zambo. He straightens his sleeve. "At what time did you arrive and notice the break-in?"

"I feed my birds every morning at five. Without fail," says De Luz.

Zambo arches his brow. "You waited before calling us?"

"Wait until you see what they did to my store. I've worked too hard to have this happen to me," says De Luz. "But," he says, "my café comes first. These little shits want to break in and destroy my store, fine, I can deal with that, but not before my café." De Luz lolls his tongue around the end of his smoke. His eyes, sleepless and bloodshot, sit tiny in his face. "I can make some if you like. Would you? It'd be no trouble."

Zambo softens.

"No. Gracias," says Zambo. "I have mine in the car."

"In the car?" De Luz makes a face like he's never heard of such a thing, leaving café in the car.

"You haven't touched anything, have you?" asks Zambo. "If you didn't disturb the evidence, we can still catch these guys."

De Luz leans towards Zambo. "Do you really think you can find the people who did this? Do you? Because I believe you can. And that is the most important thing, isn't it? For me to *believe* you can?"

"I'll do my best," says Zambo, not sure what to make of the old man.

"Before nine," says De Luz.

"Stranger things have happened," says Zambo.

"They always do," says De Luz. He tosses his cigarette to the ground and slaps his hands together. "Now, let's go."

Zambo follows De Luz around the building and De Luz points to a dumpster pushed against the back wall. Zambo follows the downspout of a rain gutter up to a window that's been smashed through. Zambo squints and sees feathers caught at the corners, airy and tufted together.

"Kids," says De Luz. "One went in and opened the door for the rest of them. Come. I'll show you."

The front of Aves en Cuando is a large industrial roll-up set to the left of a small doorway. De Luz pushes open the door and daylight falls along the entrance like a floor mat. Zambo smells feed and dust and the scent of it roots around behind his eyes.

De Luz walks into the shop and disappears into the ink. "Hold your breath," he says.

Zambo hears a click and a mechanical cranking. The roll-up lifts and releases waves of straw and feathers, impossible oceans of dust. Zambo coughs until he thinks he's going to die. Sunlight pours in and colors the room. He opens his eyes and there, in the sun-tinted haze, sees the ghost of his father.

De Luz slaps Zambo on the back.

"Take it easy, man. Look at me." De Luz pounds his chest and blows himself up. Exhales like a bellow. "Breathe like you mean it," he says. "Look what they did to my store."

Zambo shakes the vision loose, takes in the cages.

Wrought iron beauties with rounded play-tops hanging from the ceiling. Tall cages, segmented like apartment buildings. Cages the size of shoeboxes, made of chicken wire and stacked atop one another. Enormous mesh crates set on casters and made mobile. Every last one smashed open, laid to waste.

"They took everything," says De Luz.

"Not everything," says Zambo. He makes out a path around the cages to where his father was standing. Zambo bends to his knee and lifts a tiny bird, all yellow save for some white.

"Mi viejita," says De Luz. "You stayed."

Zambo hands the bird to De Luz.

"She's one of my favorites," says De Luz. "Almost ten years old," he says. "Maybe she was too old to fly? What do you think?"

"Maybe she wouldn't know where to go," says Zambo.

"Or maybe she really loves it here," says De Luz.

Zambo removes a notebook from his pocket, resumes his reason for being here. "How much you think the birds were worth?" he asks.

"Nothing," says De Luz, "I had a few that I showed at competitions but even those weren't worth anything. You know what I'd do?" De Luz licks his lips and moves in close to Zambo. "I'd dye the water, and give it to the canaries. It changed the color of the feathers. I was cheating every time."

"And you got away with it?" asks Zambo.

"They loved my birds so much. They wanted to believe they were real," says De Luz. He looks at the bird in his hand. She climbs along his arm, onto his shoulder, and begins picking at his neck and ear.

"You think whoever took them would try to sell them?" asks Zambo.

"Sell them?"

"It's a lot of birds."

"Canaries, mostly. I love canaries." De Luz takes the bird from his shoulder, grips her firmly, rubs the top of her head with his thumb.

"How much do you think someone would sell the canaries for?"

"No," says De Luz. "I know who did this. It was the neighborhood shits that come by after school. They broke in, destroyed my store, and let the birds out. Don't ask me why they did it. They're kids."

"We'll need to include the birds in the report."

"Forget the birds," says De Luz. "Find the shits who did this, and find my register. If I am to open for business I need my cash register."

Zambo turns around. On the front desk he sees a display of energy drinks tossed over, cartons of cigarettes torn open, a lesser layer of dust where the register used to sit.

"I had thirty-five dollars in the register," says De Luz. "I want that back too. All in rolled coins. I already made my weekly trip to the bank for change and I'm not about to go again."

"And this?" asks Zambo. He points towards the cages, to where he saw his father.

"To hell with that," says De Luz. "What do I need cages for without any birds?" He looks at the bird in his hand. "Isn't that right, viejita?" He lifts the bird towards his mouth, kisses her, then tosses her into the air.

*

Carlos Zambo was sixteen when his father died. He was driving home from his job at the downtown post office when a heart attack seized his breathing. He slammed the gas, crashed through a pair of parked cars and into a light post. At the funeral, everyone told Zambo he'd be the man of the house now, that his mother would need him more than ever. He nodded, said the things you say at funerals. But deep inside himself, just beyond the heartache, he felt something wholly new, breeding like mosquitoes in warm water. What he felt was a growing sense of duty, of obligation. People were counting on him. His mother was counting on him. His father, even in death, was counting on him.

During the eulogy the pastor explained how this was all part of God's plan. For so long Augustine and Violeta Zambo had worked to have a child. Doctor visits. Hormone treatments. Nothing seemed to work. Then, by the grace of our Lord and Savior, Violeta, well into her forties, was blessed with child. Carlos Ephraim Zambo. A miracle child. Brought into this world when his family least expected. And now, with his father having entered the great afterlife and Carlos entering adulthood, the Lord's plan had finally come to fruition. Carlos would be the solace his mother needs, a living reminder of the love she once shared with her husband, and a lesson in the ever-abiding power of faith.

Zambo's mother reached for her son's hand. "It's true," she said. "It's incredible what a little faith can do."

Soon after the funeral, Zambo's mother began her slide into dementia. With no one to tend to, with no routine to keep her grounded, her mind slipped right out from beneath her. When Zambo turned twenty, he moved her into a nearby nursing home where he promised to keep an eye on her, to see her every day. Soon, every day became every other day, and then every other week, and then the time between visits stretched so long it almost felt like forever.

At twenty-one, Zambo went to work for City of Miami Police. He shaved his head and his arms, grew a goatee and wore a rosary beneath his uniform.

Six months later, with Zambo green as a plátano, he and his partner Valdivia, thirty-four and trembling with alcoholism, got into a foot race with a teen suspected of robbing the Suds 'N Duds on Northwest 36th. Zambo and Valdivia were parked at Todos Jugos across the street and Zambo, fueled by his newfound sense of responsibility, gave chase. The suspect, Souleymane Taylor, a senior running back at Miami Jackson and two-time All-American, bolted past the Family Dollar, past the twenty-four-hour sandwich stand. He then leapt onto the fire escape at D'Kar Auto and Storage and was halfway to the roof when Valdivia, panicked and exhausted, fired a warning into the air. The shot must've frightened Taylor because he lost his grip, fell, and bounced his head on the pavement.

"He's going to be okay," said Valdivia. "Tell me he's going to be okay."

Zambo looked at his partner and, for a thunderclap of a moment, saw the ghost of his father. He placed his hand on Valdivia's shoulder. "He's going to be okay," said Zambo, then turned to vomit.

The following morning, Zambo called his mother. He thought he'd explain what happened before she saw it on the news—he'd be busted down to beat cop, of that he was certain, but at least he'd duck the hurricane of shit hurtling towards Valdivia. All she wanted to talk about, however, was his father. Zambo, convinced that his vision the night before was merely a result of the shock, reminded her that his father had been dead five years now. His mother said she had no idea what he was saying. His father was alive and well and sitting beside her on the bed. "He says to tell you not to worry about the boy. He's in good hands," she said.

Zambo asked to speak to Carmita.

"Has she been taking her medicine?" he asked.

"She's getting smarter about hiding it. You should see the things she does."

"When was the last time you were certain?"

"Just shy of opening her mouth and shoving it down there, I'm never certain."

"She needs her meds, Carmen."

"She needs lots of things, Carlito."

Zambo hung up the phone and tried envisioning the world his mother lived in.

*

Zambo pulls up parallel to the sidewalk. He walks along a tall metal fence until he finds the gate and lets himself in. The house is wide, Mediterranean style, and the lawn is dotted with rusting patio furniture. A van sits on the property, the name of the nursing home printed on its side in black vinyl stickers.

Inside he finds Carmita, the tallest thing he's ever seen. "I'm happy you're here," she says. "But today isn't a good day. She's refusing her medicine again."

Zambo knocks on the door to his mother's room and his mother, sitting in her rocker, comes alive. Her face is cherubic and alert. Her eyes are chandeliers, elaborate displays of glass and light. Her hair is bed-flat, and she wears a housecoat with a thin sweater over the top of it.

Zambo sits on the bed and touches her arm. "I'm happy to see you," he says.

"But you were just here yesterday," she replies. "You smother me too much."

"Carmita says you're not taking your medicine."

"Carmita? Now that's a name I haven't heard in ages."

"You forget things without your medicine," says Zambo.

"But I remember things too," she says. "Things you couldn't dream of."

Zambo pretends to believe his mother, sees his chance.

"I saw Papi today," he says. "But he wasn't quite himself."

"He said the same thing about you. Is everything okay?" she asks.

"I don't know what he wants," says Zambo. "He comes and goes and I never know why."

"Well, that does sound like your father," she says. "Always flitting around. Like a bird." She pauses. "Like a canary. Yes, like a canary. They're such pretty little birds. They've been flying by my window all day. Do you think they're the ones from this morning?"

"This morning?" asks Zambo.

"And the viejito's register? Were you able to find it?"

"We found a cellphone," says Zambo. "Two kids have already admitted to breaking in, but no, no register."

"You'll find it soon. I know you will," she says.

"How did you know about the register?" asks Zambo.

"Your father told me."

"Are you sure you're talking to Papi?" asks Zambo. "Are you absolutely sure?"

"Don't you believe me?" she asks. "Look. Here he comes now." She points outside her window. A canary settles on a clothesline, chirps once, twice, and flies away.

"Mom," says Zambo.

"Look," she says. "Can't you see how happy he is? He has so many things he wants to say to you."

Zambo looks at his mother, sees straight through to the bottom of her. She believes every word that she says.

"You're right," says Zambo. "There he is. It's like seeing him for the first time."

# 95 SPIN
## Ian Vasquez
### I-95

E veryone piles into the old Thunderbird, Shane at the wheel, you in the front, and Mario, Chris and Janine in the back. The second the tires hit I-95, Chris says, "Let's go to niggertown," and it leaves you open-mouthed, this coming from the half-Indian, half-Portuguese from Trinidad, the darkest one among you. No one calls him on it, what he thinks might be a joke; you all let it slide as you've let slide study habits and temperance during these months of mayhem that you've been hanging out together. They got a convenience store on 60th that sells beer like extra cheap, he says. How they turn a profit, don't ask me, but who are we to complain?

So it's decided—60th Street will be the first stop of the night, the heart of Liberty City, where none of you has ever spent more than the five minutes it takes to swoop into the projects behind the gas station on 62nd Street and pick up a dime bag on a night when your high-grade stash has run dry. You think of this summer as temporary neglect—but Shane has dropped out of college and has been bouncing between restaurant jobs; you, after scraping your way toward a degree on the six-year plan, flunked out last semester and have kept it a secret; Chris and Janine, the on-again-off-again couple, dropped out together this year; and Mario, the math whiz, is the only one still in school. He's the reason you're all partying tonight. His father died suddenly last week of a heart attack, just a year after emigrating from Brazil and moving into a new house in Kendall. I'm tired of hearing people crying around me, Mario had said. I got to get out of this house. So you all decided to take him out for the night, enjoy life. For you there's another reason: your girlfriend, Haley, the first girl about whom you can say you lust after *and* admire, someone it's easy to envision a future with. She's a senior at the University of Florida and is in town tonight for her sister's bachelorette splash at the Sparrow Café in the Grove, and you want to surprise her.

The quick stop in Liberty City is a success, $9.99 for a twelve-pack of Corona—how is it possible! And since you're the only one who goes into the store you take the opportunity to pick up a small box of ribbed Trojans. You remove the packets, throw away the box. A light rain begins to fall when the car pulls out of the parking lot and, by the time you merge into the traffic on 95, music is pounding, Chris is rolling a fat one, and the beers have been cracked open. Drinking and driving, one of your favorite pastimes. The beer makes the long hauls easier in this sprawling unwalkable city. Cars are zooming, despite the rain. The bright lights, the sensory overload of speed and signs and billboards and medians and walls and exit ramps. After all these years since your family left the Caribbean, Miami's still got the power to stun you. So crowded and relentless and in-your-face. The crisscrossing ribbons of highway with people rushing past each other in metal boxes still strike you as alien sometimes. Shane's needle touches ninety, needlessly. Everyone starts throwing out destinations. Someone shouts, the Tavern in the Grove, and with your ulterior motive named Haley, you second that motion loudly. Shane bellows, Grove here we come!

And that's when it happens. He changes lanes and the car swerves and fishtails and rockets into a violent spin. Spins and spins, around and around on the wet asphalt and you realize in a deep and silent place inside you that it's true what you've heard, that time slows *waaay* down. Median, barrier wall, headlights, median, barrier wall, headlights. In this suspension of time, as you wait for the brutal contact, all is peace and quiet. Music must have been playing, but the only sound you'll remember is the voice inside your head, *Please, please, don't let it hurt too bad.*

Then it's all over. The car has spun to a stop across two lanes in the middle of the highway. Cars in front and behind have braked to a stop. You cannot *believe* this. You all look at each other in amazement. Quickly Shane straightens the car out and continues driving, blithely, and everyone bursts into laughter, joy and relief, and what's more, what's so fucking incredible as to restore one's faith in the universe, Chris' arms are locked in the position of rolling the *j* and nothing has spilled, not a single sticky leaf. Now, *that* is skill, a stoner's excellence which sets the tone for the night, and the revelry takes you high and fast into the Grove.

At the Tavern you all land a table in the back corner by the jukebox and proceed with a pitcher of Bass Ale, then another. The place is noisy and hazy with smoke, cozily beautiful with everyone huddled around the table, people squeezing past, sloshing and spilling their beers and bumping into you, but it's cool, it's all good, you're here for the crush, the tunes, the distraction, to get outside yourselves and cheer Mario up. Look at him, grinning with glassy eyes.

It's all cool, except for Shane, shoving past people with another pitcher of Bass, wearing a scowl you've seen before. Often when he drinks, he gets volatile, picks up on imaginary slights and insults. Across the table Janine is commiserating with Mario, and Chris and Shane are deep in another one of their sports arguments. Jesus Christ, grow up already, you want to shout at them.

Because you have realized, with a stab of clarity, that you do not want to be there anymore. You have not touched your third glass of beer. Tonight it has no taste. You realize that you don't want this anymore—*this*—getting mindlessly intoxicated again, and so you stand up from the table and steady yourself against the chair. You're twenty-four years old and you have wasted so much time. Grow up? You were talking to *yourself*. You stumble through the crowd and the noise to the men's room, where you splash cold water on your face. You could've died out on that highway tonight. You need to see Haley, you want to smell her hair and be with her in some quiet place and talk, just talk. You want assurance that she will not leave you behind. When you head back outside, Shane's argument has turned heated—with people at the other table. He and a guy in a Marlins cap are jawing back and forth, and you ask the others, What's going on? And everyone just shakes their heads, looking uncomfortable. You tell them you're going to the Sparrow Café, you'll be right back, and make your way through the crowd and onto rain-cooled Grand Avenue.

The Sparrow's crowd is sparse, mostly older folks on the lower terrace, so you take the elevator upstairs where you expect the bachelorette party to be in full swing. But no such luck. Multicolored lights strobe the empty dance floor of the clubroom. The bartender tells you, yeah, there was a party, but it wrapped up an hour ago maybe? At the elevator you meet the café's owner—Ralph? Ray?—you've met him before through a friend who is a bar-back there. He's a tall, good-looking Italian from New York and cocky as hell. He has a bottle of wine in his hand, waiting for the elevator to open. He lives in a fancy apartment on the fourth floor. He recognizes you, treats you to an uptick of the chin. What's up, man? he says. Partying?

Trying, you say. He looks at you closely, and you know your eyes are bloodshot but you couldn't give a shit right now, and you're so busy wondering where Haley is that you step into the elevator absentmindedly.

Going up? he says, and presses the button.

Actually, no, you say, but I guess I'll take the ride, and you both smile and lean back against the wall.

He says, Dude, there's this fox upstairs waiting for me, I can't believe my *luck*. Had my eye on this one for a long time.

Yeah? and you nod with indifference.

Might as well just go ahead and satisfy her, what you think? Should I just *plunge* ahead? He gives you a mischievous smile, and you want to squirm with discomfort. Hey, he says, you wouldn't happen to have some protection with you, would you? Tonight, I'm completely unprepared. Help a brother out?

You don't know why you do it—maybe to impress him, maybe to shut him up—but you shrug and reach into your pocket and give this guy you don't really like one of your Trojans.

Hey, he says, thanks, man. And *she*—he points up—thanks you.

The elevator bucks to a stop, the door opens and he swaggers out, down the dim hallway, and over his shoulder you see a girl waiting at a door, and he says, Why didn't you go in? and the girl says, I don't mind waiting. And her voice startles you.

You hold back the doors, step forward and peer out, and she glances past him, then swivels her shoulder away and lets her blonde hair fall to the side, curtaining her face.

Haley. It's Haley. You hit the button, the doors close and the elevator takes you down down down.

You follow your feet back to the Tavern and the street sounds are noises from a distant star. Your chest feels like it's going to burst. Your only solace is you didn't lose your cool. Had you confronted her, you would've surely lost it, but you held on to your dignity. You're devastated, you can't focus, and then you see blood on the sidewalk and Mario standing in the crowd in front of the Tavern and Shane slumped against the wall. His nose and mouth are bleeding.

He and that guy got into it, Mario says.

Where's Chris and Janine?

Mario rolls his eyes and gestures vaguely. They left. She said Chris made a pass at somebody and now they're fighting.

You and Mario take Shane home in his car, you driving, Mario in shotgun and Shane sprawled in the back. You weave and zip through traffic on U.S. 1 and bank onto 95, the Thunderbird responsive and smooth at eighty miles per. You tap the pedal. Ninety. You lower the windows and the wind rushes in with the smell of rain and sky. You can't stop thinking about her and you want to get away from this pain. From this aimless life you're leading. Ninety-five miles an hour, now you're flying into the future. Mario looks at you with wonderment and alarm. One hundred.

A few years up the road, you will lose all of tonight's friendships. Shane will develop a coke habit and one night, after a three-day binge, will suffer a seizure and suffocate facedown in his pillow at age twenty-seven. Chris and Janine will marry and divorce after two years. Chris will return to Trinidad, fail at a business venture, and end his life with exhaust fumes one Christmas Eve in his mother's garage. Last you'll hear of Janine: rehab somewhere in California.

Mario will escape unscathed, to a job in Virginia with GE, but you won't hear from him. And Haley?

One hundred ten. You've got to believe the tires will hold, that you won't spin out again, that you'll whoosh on through and slide safely through the curves. You've got to believe that the road will take care of you, that you'll exit this rain-slick patch and roar off the highway through one green light and the next and the next, and tomorrow you'll awake with your heart exquisitely broken, but you'll be all right, you'll be fine, because speed like this, one hundred fifteen, can be scary and unpredictable, with the breeze so strong it brings tears to your eyes, but it makes you feel something, this pain is yours. It makes you feel *alive*.

*15 Views of Miami*

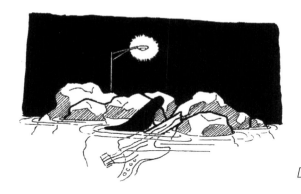

# BISCAYNE
Patricia Engel
*Downtown, Biscayne Corridor*

You waited out Hurricane Andrew huddled on the floor of a closet with your brother and mother in the Miami Lakes rental your father left you all with before his sentencing for dealing. Your mother had waited a decade for him, you all had, but he decided to make his freshly paroled life with another woman, a neighbor you'd once called tía. Your Papi died in that storm, when he went out to move his new lady's car away from the very palm that crushed him. I was across the county in West Kendall that night. With my parents, still healthy, my sister, still living, curled on the mattresses our father had laid out so we could pretend we were camping. I was fifteen. You, seventeen. We wouldn't meet for a decade but that night I knew. I knew you.

It's all so different now. I often drive past our old place on Biscayne. Our building, that two-story cement cube, a lone decrepit relic in the undertow of towering metal beasts. Our neighbors' bungalows and buildings were bought, knocked down, and replaced with luxury high-rises. Our landlord, that stubborn bastard, has held out, letting the ground floor shop tenants pay the same old rent. The barber is still there. Tino's bodega on the corner. The laundromat. Our apartment is still there too, though I heard it stayed empty for a while after we left. Our window, the half-moon that brought sun and starlight into our living room, was broken for months, covered by a cardboard sheath, and months later, the glass pane was finally replaced. We'd watch the boulevard from that window, from the Bacardi Building to Out of the Closet. The teenagers selling coke and pills on the corner, ignored by cops, and occasional tourists, lost after a wrong turn from Bayside and the cruise ships. We watched the summer rain hammer the street below. We boarded its frame with plywood when the hurricanes came. You kissed me many times by that window. We'd fall naked together on our wooden floor or drag ourselves into our small bedroom, to your old futon. We never got around to buying a real bed. I was sad to see it out on the curb when you left.

Sometimes I turn in on our corner of 25th just to see what's happened to our block, drive slow toward the bay. I get out of my car and walk to our spot just beyond the railing, where the rocks bleed into water. You told me you loved me on those rocks. It was out of jealousy, after you'd seen me receptive to a stranger's flirting earlier that night at I/O. You'd pulled me out of the club with urgency, driven me to the embankment and said, your voice quaking, that you didn't know what we were meant to be to one another. Just that tonight it was love and tomorrow it would be love too.

The night we met at Piccadilly's, you touched my arm as I passed you in the crowd. I know you, you said. I shook my head. I *do*, you insisted, and that was all it took. Piccadilly's is still there but was sold to a series of new owners and is now a clothing boutique. That was when the Design District was a destination only if you wanted to get jumped. My father warned me against going there. He'd become much more protective since my mother passed. He thought he could save his daughters from the harm of strangers, this city's wild fists. You were with me a year later at my sister's funeral. You drove me around for months afterward, to and from work, always taking the long way on the side roads because I was afraid, so afraid, that like my sister I'd die at the hands of a reckless driver in a stolen car flying down I-95.

You worked at Target on upper Biscayne in those days, one of the first to pop up in the city. You sold electronics, TVs to couples and bachelors, CD players and mixers to other musicians. You missed work regularly to rehearse for gigs. Your band was doing well, with a dedicated following, playing all over South Florida and sometimes in other states. People often asked what you guys were still doing in this town, why you didn't try your luck in Atlanta or New York. They say talent always leaves Miami, our own diaspora, but you were defiant, wore the 305 with pride, said you'd never leave the land that made you, that made me.

One Noche Buena with my father, when we were celebrating with aguardiente that your band, after months of A & R courtship, had finally been signed to a major label, Papi took me aside and told me the worst thing that could happen to us was your success. I didn't understand what he meant. Later he would clarify: There will be women, mi'jita, many women, and a distance that will drive you into the sea. My father lived in his own tomb of sadness since cancer ripped my mother away, since losing my sister, so I didn't listen to him.

The next Noche Buena, you were in Buenos Aires, your band a new fixture on the Rock En Español scene. You were nominated for three Latin Grammys, featured in magazines, doing radio interviews every other day. All the Lincoln

Road girls of MTV and Sony Latin wanted to sleep with any one of you in the band. You played bass and they whispered this meant you were gifted with your fingers. They didn't care that you loved me. They laughed at me when I turned my back. You said to ignore them. You said you loved nobody, no body, but me and mine.

We used to get our hair dyed black together by the transvestite in the barbershop downstairs. You bought me a cafecito at the Latin Café every morning, and we had dinners of croquetas or empanadas there most nights, or just ate bar food with your buddies at Churchill's or Tobacco Road. Now there are gourmet food trucks up and down the boulevard, and some fancier restaurants have migrated from South Beach. The dingy pockets of our former territory now go by neighborhoody names, designated as districts, and are written about in travel magazines. The desolate warehouse ward where your band rehearsed has turned into a full-fledged gallery zone with its own yuppie art walk. I think you would smile to see the city you loved, but lost your faith in, change around us.

I wanted to go to law school. I wanted to fight for the rights of immigrants, use my Spanish for advocacy. Something like that. It's vague to me now though those were plans I'd held since childhood, promises I'd made to my mother. One night on our rocks, the place we always went for our hard conversations, the clouds covered the moon and the bay water lost its shine. I couldn't see your face but knew it so well, your stars for pupils, the way you turned away your gaze when you knew you were about to hurt me. There's not room in your dreams for both of us, you said. I asked what you meant but you couldn't say. I only knew that by the next breath my ambitions felt cheap and I was ready to betray them. I don't need to be a lawyer, I said, suddenly hating my education, the one my parents worked so hard to provide. I would follow you anywhere,

I said, because I knew the other guys and your new manager had put in your ear that Miami was too small for your band now; it was time to move to Los Angeles or Mexico City, where Latin bands go to bloom.

You had this idea that I was a fragile thing. You didn't like when I walked out to my car alone at night even though there were only thirteen stairs to our patch of curb on Biscayne, and just a few more steps to reach my Camry. You didn't like when I stopped to talk to Jo, the Texan prostitute who worked our block, even though she was always the first to say hi. Sometimes, when you weren't around, she would buy me a Fresca in the bodega and we'd stand together while she smoked a cigarette. She'd say, as if I'd been the one to ask, I'm going to get out of this place one day soon. This boulevard ain't right for nice girls like you and me.

One night when you were out rehearsing, I pulled up in front of our building and saw Jo on the corner, dancing like a little girl at a recital. Beside her, a guy in a wheelchair with a crumpled body, stumps for legs folded into his tiny torso, one nubby arm and one longer one reached out, holding her hand like she was his prize. She was dancing for him and, by the way she looked at him tenderly, it was easy to forget he was her job for the next hour or two. I told you about it when you came home that night. I smelled the sweat and weed on you as you pulled off your t-shirt and stepped out of your jeans.

When we were finished making love, you told me you'd decided with the other guys on a December departure. Lalo, the drummer, had a cousin in LA with an apartment you could crash in till you got settled and you'd start looking for a place for the two of us to share right away. I was working in a lawyer's office in the Gables and you suggested I move back in with my father to save money.

You'd come back for me in a few months, you said. We'd take my car and cross the country together, maybe even get married in Vegas on the way. I wanted to be angry that you'd made the decision to go without me, but I knew if I hadn't already lost you, I would right then.

Papi was already sick. He didn't want anyone to know. I shouldn't have been surprised because when my mother died, I couldn't imagine him living very long without her. Theirs was a love that seemed its own sacrament. That's the love I wanted. The love I thought we're all entitled to have. I didn't yet know, because we hadn't yet been tested, that you and I were different about loyalty. Your mother cried when you were leaving, yet you did not flinch. My father didn't offer more than a nod when I announced I would soon leave to join you, but it was enough for me to understand that no matter how much I wanted to go, I never would.

We didn't say goodbye by the rocks, as we should have. I was there just last night, walking over the uneven paving, passing the band of stray cats weaving through the parked cars. I took my place on the other side of the metal divider that keeps people from driving into the water. Bodies have washed up on those rocks. We used to joke about the knack for Miami waters to spit up floppy dead hands or severed feet. Sometimes we'd pick up a washed-up shirt and wonder about its origins. Dropped off a fishing boat, or maybe ripped by waves from the back of a balsero. We'd walk back to our apartment slowly, toward the rush of traffic and street folk along the concrete corridor, our hands deep in each other's butt pockets, leaning into each other's shoulders. We'd look up at the white shard of moon hanging low like a broken chandelier and whisper to one another, with the solemnity of a vow, This moon is our moon, this boulevard is our boulevard.

# FROM THE DESK OF DAVID J. HERNANDEZ, SECURITY OFFICER, WESTLAND MALL

## Jennine  Capó Crucet

### *Hialeah*

August 7, 1998


Dear To Whom It May Concern:

    My name is David J. Hernandez, and I am a security officer with Platinum Number One Protection. I am writing on my own behalf, not as an employee of Platinum but as someone who cares a lot (very much) about safety and the law. I take my job as the security at Westland Mall really seriously, partly because soon, I hope to someday be a Dade County Police Officer once I pass the GED. Therefore, I see patrolling Westland Mall as being on the road of my path to success. So first off, please hear me when I say that I appreciate the opportunity to serve and protect this Mall and its citizens. I want to say also how much I enjoy patrolling Westland Mall because I enjoy the Mall atmosphere, and also the unique wood paneling on the ceilings and the fact that there are so many huge skylights, so I can tell if it's day still or if it's night already—-which isn't the case at other malls and so makes

Westland very unique. Also, Picadilly's by the Sears is pretty good and they give me free desserts during my shifts. Also, I also appreciate the girls at Burdines letting me park the golf cart inside the store sometimes, which is very sweet of them, especially when it's raining. These are just some of the many great things about serving and protecting here.

Now as we are all aware, Back To School Shopping Season is upon us, and that means Westland Mall will have a severely large intake of customers, especially those that are teenagers and even younger, with and without parents. In light of this, I respectfully submit this report in the hopes of making this Mall the best and safest in South Florida. (And also showing my commitment and also because I want to show that I have what it takes!)

With that in mind, I looked over the Suggested Safety Tips For Shopping at Westland Mall, along with the Mall's Behavioral Code of Conduct. Copies of both are in the security office AKA headquarters, but these documents should be more visually available to potential perpetrators——this is, by the way, my first suggestion.

Basically and first of all, it is my professional opinion that Westland Mall needs to put something in the Safety Tips (and on signs upon entering the Mall via the various entrances) about not feeling pressure to give money to disabled people (i.e. "bums," etc.) in wheelchairs who hang out by the Mall entrances. Now, I am aware that it is part of my job to report those who are loitering and soliciting by the entrances to the "actual" authorities should a perpetrating loiterer refuse to leave, but the thing is they almost ALWAYS **do** refuse to leave, and it is usually up to half an hour before other authorities can come, so that's like thirty or more minutes that they're still there, asking for money.

I can't always stay there to encourage incoming Mall patrons to walk by and not feel bad about not giving him money. (NOTE: I say "him" because it is almost ALWAYS this one guy—-this guy in this wheelchair—-who told me he used to panhandle over at Zayre but got harassed by cops there and so now he harasses Westland Mall and I am convinced the stumps that he has instead of legs freak people out and this RUINS their enjoyment of the Mall experience). If citizens entering the Mall are made aware, via proper signage, that they can just ignore this dude and his wheelchair and that they are free to not make eye contact with his stumps, it is my professional opinion that this signage would improve community relations.

(FYI: I've tried to tell him he's loitering but he says he's read the Code of Conduct and he knows it basically by heart, and basically, he proved he's got as much right to be there as anyone else, and based on the letter of the law he is right. Which is why I think the above-mentioned signage would help and at least discourage him from showing up.)

Which brings me to my suggestions about The Code of Conduct. First of all, I think there really needs to be some more specific thing in there about the fountains. I am CONSTANTLY having to tell parents to get their kids out of the fountains. I am CONTANSTLY having to kick teenagers out of the Mall because they steal the coins out of the fountains. And the truth is, I'm doing this based on what is basically my really loose interpretation of the rule regarding disturbing others AKA "boisterous activity" (Rule No.3 in the current Code of Conduct). If there were a legit rule about not messing with the fountains, I'd have more authority when doing this, and would not have people questioning me or saying I'm overreacting when I ask them to please exit a fountain. The exact wording should of course be left up to you (or probably lawyers?), though even a simple DO NOT ENTER OR LOITER IN THE FOUNTAINS would be good.

Also, in fact it is my strong feeling that, maybe we need some sort of fencing around these fountains? I get that it would ruin the look of them, but maybe there's a way to make it look good? Because basically on Friday nights and Saturdays I'd say that like 85% of my incident reports mention *something* regarding the fountains. Also, half the time there isn't even water in the fountains (not sure how come ((??)) but also: it's not my business) and sometimes older patrons—mostly old ladies—-ask me *why* there's no water, and I don't know what to say. I used to just say "I don't know" but then I figured out that undermined my authority with the patrons, so now I say that I'm not authorized to relay that information, which sometimes (by accident) freaks them out.

Also—-and I debated even bringing this up, so please do not consider this disrespectful and/or me saying how to run this Mall—-but I think there needs to be better enforcement/regulation/whatever of Rule No. 9 concerning, and I quote, "Any form of solicitation or distributing handbills, leaflets, commercial advertising or promotional material of any kind without prior written permission of Mall Management."

Basically, I think you guys know where I'm going with this.

Basically, I'm talking about the girls from John Casablanca's School of Modeling and Career Center, who as we are all aware have been giving us some problems as of lately.

I understand that their presence has been approved by Mall Management, and while I respect this, I believe it should be reconsidered after the events at the end of this past month (i.e. July) with regards to that one model-in-training attempting to "recruit" those twin sisters who then perpetrated boisterous activity against said model-in-training (i.e. in the form of the VERY loud jingle one of the twins made up ON THE SPOT and then SANG, and which went——more or less, and I quote——"John Casablanca! Where you PAY to Be A Model! Then They MAKE You Stand Around in the MAAAAAALL!" And then the other twin pushed said model-in-training into the above-mentioned fountain, which FYI, **did** have water in it at that moment, and therefore resulted in an accidental slip-and-fall liability).

Don't get me wrong: Sometimes the models from John Casablanca's School of Modeling look like real actual models, and that means, because it is partly my job to protect their safety, that I am ***extremely*** grateful for this opportunity. But we have turned a blind ear to their disturbances for way too long, and therefore it is with a heavy load that I feel it my duty to inform the Mall Management: Those girls are NO GOOD, always fighting with each other, always behaving in ways that anger and annoy other Mall citizens. If their presence were not sanctioned by Mall Management, they would be the first people I'd escort from the premises——though probably after the gangbanger types (see Rule No.14) and those super loud super-chusma girls in their overalls and tube tops, always taking off their hoop earrings while picking fights (see Rule No.6), fights that are basically just extensions of whatever they already fought over earlier that week at Hialeah High (no offense——I can say that because I went there even though I didn't graduate, so that's why——GO THOROUGHBREDS!!).

Also, sometimes those John Casablanca's girls, because they're wearing high heels, they take off their shoes and walk around, their bare feet red and covered in blisters right there on the public floor. Which puts them in IMMEDIATE violation of Rule No.3. And when I try to very politely ***but with my sanctioned authority*** warn them about this-—when I ask that they please remove their bare feet from the tile and put back on their shoes-—they commit one or more obscene gestures, both to my face and behind my back (including calling me "Loser" and/or "Freaking Loser" and also actual obscene words that I won't even write here out of respect for Mall Management). And the use of obscenities is CLEARLY-—I don't even need to say this-—a CLEAR violation of Rule No.1.

So if we actually want to follow the letters of the law, I urge Mall Management to think deeply about possibly not granting written permission to the solicitationing of John Casablanca's in the future. Westland Mall and its other citizens (non-models, security, etc.) deserve ***and should get*** this respect.

In summary, I would like to say that in my time here at Westland Mall, Westland Mall has experienced a significant reduction in thefts, particularly from Specs Music and Burdines, two establishments which prior to now were infamous for their rates of shoplifting. This isn't at ALL a complaint, but I am sometimes the ONLY security personnel on a shift for the ENTIRE Mall and surrounding parking areas. It is a hard job, a tough job, but good preparation for the real world and for the challenges I will face as an Officer of the Law.

Please do not think I have overstepped my bounds in supplying you with these observations and suggestions. If I have, I sincerely apologize. But still, this report comes out of concern and commitment and love for the city of Hialeah and this, its greatest Mall.

On a personal note, I've been coming to Westland Mall—as I like to say—since I was a sperm. No joke, my parents met at this Mall. I've brought every girl I've ever tried to get with to this Mall at some point. I've bought her a pizza slice and a garlic knot at the Sbarro. I've carried our tray to a table near the back wall of the Food Court, and after, I've sat with each of them at the fountain by the Sears and laughed at the little kids squatting to pee, at their parents ripping them from the water. I truly look forward to bringing my future family here someday. To experiencing, as a someday Officer of the Law, all this Mall has to offer. I look forward to being a credit to the place that raised me, a credit to this Mall that I too have peed upon and now ***all these years later*** serve and protect.

I trust that in response to these words, Mall Management will govern itself accordingly. I appreciate your time and consideration. I have the upmost faith that moving forward together we will continue to make Westland Mall all it can be.

Respectfully submitted,
David J. Hernandez, Security Officer, Westland Mall
Future Police Officer Dade County
(AKA DJ Joey Lawless – Quinces/Proms/House Parties/Mall Events – page me 4 detail$$$)

*15 Views of Miami*

# JAMOKES
## John Dufresne
### *Ojus*

A man with a five-inch lockback knife buried to its heel in his chest stumbles into Café Olé on West Dixie, settles into a chair, and leans his shoulder against the wall. The barista looks up from his issue of *Automundo* and sees the bleeding man. "*Puta madré*, dude! You're stabbed!"

The man says, "Can you call 911 for me and then bring me a tall vanilla latté and a straw."

The barista makes the call. The young girl, sitting at a table by the door, cries when she sees the blood splattered on the yellow knife handle and soaked into the man's FIU t-shirt. The man with her, who might be her father but is not, tells her to close her eyes and think bright thoughts.

The bleeding man coughs and moans. He asks the barista for a towel or a rag or something. "I hope you don't mind if I wait here for the ambulance. You can't even breathe out there." He's talking about the shroud of smoke from the fires in the Everglades that has settled over the county. The fires have been burning for seven days now. The bleeding man looks at the young girl and says, "Is this the end of the world, honey?"

The barista brings a towel, the latté, and a straw and sets them on the table. The man says, "I can't pay you for this."

"*La casa invita.*"

The man smiles and reaches for the towel.

"You got no hands, dude," the barista says.

The man holds up his lopped arms. "Look, Ma…"

"What happened?"

"I got stabbed."

"With your hands, I mean."

A Miami-Dade police officer walks in and speaks into the radio microphone looped to his epaulet. He's making sure the paramedics are on their way. He nods to the young girl and the man with her and stops at the bleeding man's table. The girl and the man slip their disposable facemasks over their mouths and noses and leave the café. The officer looks at the knife and whistles. "What happened to you, partner?"

The barista says, "He got stabbed."

"Not talking to you."

"Just trying to help."

"Back the fuck off, José!"

"Rafael," the barista says.

The bleeding man says, "Flesh-eating bacteria."

"No, I meant the knife. Who did this to you?"

"Cecil Twitty, this guy that lives in my building and his girlfriend, Sparkle. Would you mind peeling the straw and putting it in my latté."

The officer bites the end of the paper sleeve over the straw and spits it out. He blows on the straw and shoots the sleeve in a loop across the room. He taps the straw into the drink. "And what's your name?"

"Clark Chapman. But they call me Handsome."

"That's cold."

Clark looks puzzled, but then gets it. "I see what you mean."

"Do you know where I could find Twitty and Sparkle?"

Clark points with his chin to the plate glass window. "There they are, the two jamokes, across the street in front of the Pita Hut."

*

Officer Zane Brophy asks Sparkle to take a seat in the back of his squad car while he has a word with Cecil. He calls for backup. The paramedics slide Clark onto the gurney and wheel him to the ambulance. Cecil says, "That's a hundred dollar German knife right there."

Brophy's standing over Cecil who's leaning on the trunk of the squad car. Brophy waits for the siren to fade. He says to Cecil, "Why don't you tell me what happened."

"Aren't you going to read me my rights?"

"Should I?"

"I know my rights."

"I know you do."

"Sparkle is pregnant."

"How old is she?"

"Fourteen. And a half."

"How old are you?"

"Twenty-two on Monday."

"Go on."

"Where do I start?"

"In the middle."

"Well, we need a car, need cash, need to get outta Dodge."

"You're speaking in the present tense."

"I am?"

"This leaving of Dodge will not happen."

"So I should say, 'We needed a car'?"

"But you don't anymore."

Cecil coughs black soot into his hanky. "Look at this shit we're breathing."

"So you attempted to rob Mr. Chapman."

"Sparkle's idea."

"Why him?"

"The not having hands. Can't fight back, we figured. Wrong. We were drinking this skunky Vino Once—shit smells so bad it'd knock a maggot off a honey wagon—and I whacked Handsome with the bottle. His eyes rolled back in his head and he dropped. We searched the apartment. I poured water on his face, and he shook himself awake."

Brophy stares down West Dixie, the view diminished and obscured, like looking at the world through gauzy curtains, like the curtains in what's-her-name's bedroom. Monica. His eyes burn.

Cecil says, "He told us he had no money."

"Theft 101: *Rob the rich.*"

"I punched him in the windpipe. He bit me and started barking. I stuck him and he got stronger and ran. You might wonder how a handless man can open a door." Cecil lifts his brow and smiles. "A lever, not a knob."

*

Brophy leans into the squad car and shakes Sparkle's shoulder. She wakes and asks him to turn on the AC.

"How many months along are you?"

"Along what?"

"Your pregnancy."

"I'm not pregnant."

"Where did Cecil get that idea?"

"I just needed him to do something. It's so boring here."

"He did something."

"So you found the body."

"Mr. Chapman's not dead."

"I saw that. I meant Cary Grant."

\*

Brophy sits on the curb beside Cecil. "Who's Cary Grant?"

"You know?"

"Sparkle let it slip."

"He cooked meth up in Polk County."

"Stop right there, Cecil. I'm going to Mirandize you, and then we'll take a ride to headquarters, and you can tell your story."

"Can we stop at McDonald's?"

"We'll have burgers for you at the station."

"Can I see Sparkle?"

"Probably not for the rest of your life."

\*

Brophy watches Cecil through the two-way mirror in the interview room. Cecil opens his Big Mac and takes out the pickles. He licks the sauce from the bun and puts fries on the burger because that's the way the Cubans do it. When he's finished, Detective Maninderjit Dallah enters, sits, and cleans the table with a Lysol disinfecting wipe. Cecil doesn't believe Dallah's a cop. He's never seen a cop with a turban, a beard, and a bow tie. Cecil has said he doesn't want a lawyer; he hates lawyers. Bottom feeders, he says.

"I killed Cary Grant. There was no rhyme or reason; no conscious decision was made. Just a chain of circumstances that went from bad to worse. Bad circumstance number one: I was out of dope. Bad circumstance number two: Cary was not. Number three: I had no money."

Dallah twists the *kara* on his wrist and says, "Cruelty, material attachment, greed, and anger are the four rivers of fire."

Cecil says he has to take a dump. Dallah says we'll be done shortly. Cecil says he can't wait. Dallah calls for an officer-escort, and he tells Cecil to wash his hands when he's done with his business. Warm water, soap, thirty seconds.

Brophy texts his wife and tells her he's tied up with a case and won't be home till God knows when. *Kiss the girls goodnight. XOXOX.*

When Cecil returns, he smiles and says, "That was a load off my mind."

Dallah says, "Tell me about the madness."

"I asked him nicely. I said, Cary, tell us where the dope is. He was sprawled out on the ratty couch, feet up on the coffee table, one hand in his pants, the other on the remote. He turned up the volume on the TV. I hit him on the head with the aluminum baseball bat he keeps by the front door. He stood and stepped toward me, but fell. I heard Sparkle in the kitchen going through the drawers and cabinets. I asked him again to tell me where he hid the shit. Sparkle came into the den with a plastic bag, and we tied it over his head and taped it shut. End of story."

"Did you find what you were looking for?"

"Last place we looked."

"Have you killed anyone else, Cecil?"

"What do you mean by *kill*?"

*

Brophy's at Monica Feather's condo on Key Biscayne when he gets the text that Clark Chapman has died. He rolls out of bed and pours himself a drink. He stares out the bedroom window at the distant orange glow from the Everglades fires. Monica says, "The wife tugging at your leash?"

*

The young girl says *Zoë* when the man asks her to repeat her new name. She points to the color she wants: Nice 'n Easy Extra Light Neutral Blonde. He says, "You'll look ravishing, my dear," and tells her that they still need to buy scissors and a comb. Detective Dallah's at Walgreens picking up his wife's Clozapine. He's remembering the words of the Guru: *The world is like a dream; there is nothing of it that is yours.* He wonders why the little girl is wearing her facemask inside the store and why the man keeps rubbing his forehead. What is he struggling with? Something funny going on here? The girl, whose given name is Flor, and who is five, tells the man that the guy with the turban is staring at them. The man, who calls himself Kit, takes her tiny hand in his and leads her away from the pharmacy and toward the registers up front. He's following us, Zoë says. Dallah gets a text message from Janjak, his wife's caregiver: *need Wings Quilted Overnight Pullups.* He walks to Aisle 7 and sees the man and girl leave the store. Probably nothing, he decides.

*

Kit dyes Zoë's hair in the men's room at the Valero station, dries it with paper towels. They walk to Ojus Park and sit at a picnic table by the rec center. The scissors have a finger rest on the eye ring that Kit appreciates, unnecessary but purposeful and elegant. *Culture* is everything we do that we don't have to do. He cuts her hair short, maybe too short. Tried for Michelle Williams but got Justin Timberlake. Her head seems lighter, Zoë says. What he hears is *seems slighter.* When they see Juancho, the tweaked-out sack of shit who lives with Flor's mom, heading their way, Kit tousles Zoë's hair and says, "I got this."

Juancho holds up his droopy camouflage jeans in one hand and pokes Kit in the chest with the other. "Roxy wants her little flower back." He looks at Zoë, shakes his head, says to Kit, "That's one sorry-ass disguise, amigo."

"Roxy's a crack whore." Kit can read Juancho's neck tattoo: *Game Over!*

"And I'm here to take her back, dickwad. *¡Venga, niña!*"

"You can't have her."

"Oh, I've had her."

"You ever touch this baby?"

Juancho smiles and says he's done more than touch. "Ain't that right, *caramelo?*"

Kit tells Zoë to close her eyes and think happy thoughts. She puts her arms on the table and her head in her arms. Kit drives the scissors into Juancho's throat between the *e* and the *O*. Juancho grabs for the scissors, and his trousers fall to his knees. He's gurgling blood. Kit stands and pushes on the scissors until Juancho falls to his back. Kit rolls him over. He tells Zoë that Juancho fell asleep. He holds her face in his bloody hands and says, "Zoë, you're all that matters."

*

Sparkle lies on the bed in her cell and scrapes the *plum crazy* polish off her fingernails with her thumbnail. She lied to the cops twice. About feeling sad for killing that dirtbag Grant. About not being pregnant. She thinks it's a riot how she's doing time with her own little inmate, her get-out-of-jail-free card. They'll find out soon enough, and they'll have to let her go.

*

Last night's rain put the fires out. The sun is up. The air smells like peppers. There are green and blue canaries trilling in the mango tree. Zoë snuggles under a sheet in the back seat of Kit's station wagon. They're parked on the swale outside a nursing home. Kit's up front, leaning back against the door, the breeze from the open window stirring his hair. He's reading Zoë a story about a red-haired girl in Canada. He says, "Anne came dancing home in the purple winter twilight across the snowy places." And Zoë shuts her eyes and lets herself be carried away to a sweeter world.

# ABOUT THE EDITOR

Born in Puerto Rico and raised in Miami Beach, **Jaquira Díaz** is the recipient of a Pushcart Prize, the Carl Djerassi Fiction Fellowship from the Wisconsin Institute for Creative Writing, and an NEA Fellowship to the Hambidge Center for the Creative Arts and Sciences. She's been awarded scholarships and fellowships from the Sewanee Writers' Conference, Bread Loaf, the Key West Literary Seminar, the MacDowell Colony, the Summer Literary Seminars, and *Tin House*'s Summer Writers' Workshops. Her work has been noted in *Best American Essays*, and appears in *Ploughshares*, *The Kenyon Review*, *The Sun*, *The Southern Review*, *Five Chapters*, *Salon*, and the Pushcart Prize anthology, among other publications. She is Assistant Essays Editor at *The Rumpus*, Associate Fiction Editor at *West Branch*, and host of Sunday Salon Miami. She always carries Charms Blow Pops and/or Ring Pops in her purse (in case of emergency) and she knows all the words to Slick Rick's "La Di Da Di," even the Doug E. Fresh beatbox parts.

# ABOUT THE CONTRIBUTORS

**Lynne Barrett** is the author of the story collections *Magpies* (Gold Medal, Florida Book Awards), *The Secret Names of Women*, and *The Land of Go*, and co-editor of *Birth: A Literary Companion*. Her recent work has appeared or is forthcoming in *Trouble in the Heartland: Stories Inspired by the Songs of Bruce Springsteen*, *Fort Lauderdale Magazine*, *Real South*, *Ellery Queen's Mystery Magazine*, *The Southern Women's Review*, *Delta Blues*, and *One Year to a Writing Life*. A recipient of the Edgar Award for best mystery story, she teaches in the MFA program at Florida International University and edits *The Florida Book Review*. Lynne's website is lynnebarrett.com.

**Jennine Capó Crucet** is the author of the novel *Magic City Relic* (St. Martin's Press, 2015) and the story collection *How to Leave Hialeah*, which won the Iowa Short Fiction Award, the John Gardner Prize, and the Devil's Kitchen Award in Prose. The collection was also named a Best Book of the Year by *the Miami Herald*, the *Miami New Times*, and the Latinidad List. A winner of an O. Henry Prize and a Bread Loaf Fellow, she served as the 2013/14 Picador Guest Professor of American Literature and Creative Writing at the University of Leipzig in Germany. She currently lives and teaches in Florida, but hangs out on Twitter: @crucet.

**Susanna Daniel**'s first novel, *Stiltsville*, was awarded the 2011 PEN/Bingham prize for best debut fiction, and her second novel, *Sea Creatures*, was an Amazon Best Book of the Month and a *Minneapolis Star-Tribune* Best Book of 2013. Susanna was born and raised in Miami, Florida, where she spent much of her childhood at her family's stilt house in Biscayne Bay. Susanna is a co-founder of the Madison Writers' Studio. She is a graduate of Columbia University and the University of Iowa Writers' Workshop. Her writing has been published in *Newsweek*, *Slate*, *One Story*, *Epoch*, and elsewhere. Susanna lives with her husband and two young sons in Madison, Wisconsin, where during the long winter she dreams of the sun and the sea, and of jumping off the stilt house porch at high tide. She is at work on a third novel.

**Phillippe Diederich** is a Haitian-American writer and photographer born in the Dominican Republic and raised in Mexico City and Miami. His short fiction has been awarded the 2013 Chris O'Malley Fiction Prize from *The Madison Review*, the Association of Writing Programs Intro Journal Award for fiction, and received two Pushcart nominations. His stories have appeared in *Quarterly West*, *High Desert Journal*, *Hobart*, *Frostwriting*, *The Madison Review* and many others. He is the author of *Communism and the Art of Motorcycle Maintenance*, an eBook that includes an essay and forty black and white photographs of Cuban Harley-Davidson bikers in Havana, Cuba. His first novel, *Sofrito*, will be published in the spring of 2015 by Cinco Puntos Press.

**John Dufresne** is the author of two short story collections, *The Way That Water Enters Stone* and *Johnny Too Bad*, and the novels *Louisiana Power & Light*, *Love Warps the Mind a Little*, both *New York Times* Notable Books of the Year, *Deep in the Shade of Paradise*, and *Requiem, Mass*. His books on writing, *The Lie That Tells a Truth* and *Is Life Like This?* are used in many university writing programs. He's the editor of the anthology *Blue Christmas*. His short stories have twice been named Best American Mystery Stories, in 2007 and 2010. His play *Trailerville* was produced at the Blue Heron Theater in New York in 2005. He's a professor at Florida International University in Miami. He is a 2013 Guggenheim Fellow in Fiction. His newest novel is *No Regrets, Coyote*.

**Patricia Engel** is the author of *It's Not Love, It's Just Paris* and *Vida*, which was a *New York Times* Notable Book of the Year and a finalist for the PEN/Hemingway and Young Lions Fiction Awards. Her fiction has appeared in *The Atlantic*, *A Public Space*, *Boston Review*, and *Harvard Review*, among other publications, and received numerous awards including a 2014 fellowship in prose from the National Endowment for the Arts. She lives in Miami.

Born in Port-au-Prince, **Michèle-Jessica (M.J.) Fievre** is an expat who authored several mystery novels and children's books in French, including *Sortilège Haïtien* (2011). She obtained her MFA from the Creative Writing program at Florida International University. Her short stories and poems in English have appeared in *Haiti Noir* (Akashic Books, 2011), *The Beautiful Anthology* (TNB Books, 2012), *The*

*Mom Egg, The Southeast Review*, and *The Caribbean Writer*. M.J. is the founding editor of *Sliver of Stone Magazine*, and a regular contributor to *The Nervous Breakdown*. She is also a proud member of the Miami Poetry Collective, famous for its Poem Depot, a regular feature of Wynwood's Second Saturday Art Walk. She's a Board Member of Women Writers of Haitian Descent, Inc., and edited the Haiti anthology, *So Spoke the Earth* (WWOHD, 2012). She blogs at mjfievre.com.

**M. Evelina Galang** is the author of *Her Wild American Self* (Coffee House Press, '96); the novel *One Tribe* (New Issues Press, '06); and *Angel de la Luna and the 5$^{TH}$ Glorious Mystery* (Coffee House Press 2013). She has edited the anthology, *Screaming Monkeys: Critiques of Asian American Images* (Coffee House Press, '03). She is currently writing *Lolas' House: Women Living with War*, stories of surviving Filipina WWII "Comfort Women" and is at work on a new novel, *Beautiful Sorrow, Beautiful Sky*. Galang teaches in and directs the Creative Writing Program at the University of Miami, is core faculty for VONA/Voices: Voices of Our Nation Arts Foundation, and has been named one of the 100 most influential Filipinas in the United States by Filipina Women's Network.

**Corey Ginsberg**'s writing has most recently appeared in such publications as *Third Coast, PANK, The Cream City Review, Subtropics, The Nashville Review,* and the *Potomac Review,* among others. Corey currently lives in Miami and works as a freelance writer. Her favorite thing about living in Miami is wearing shorts in February and never having to shovel snow. Ever.

**J. David Gonzalez**'s work has appeared or is forthcoming in *Thuglit, Plots With Guns, Los Angeles Review of Books, Yeti, Jai-Alai Magazine, thickjam* and elsewhere. He currently lives in Los Angeles where he works as a bookseller at Skylight Books and produces an interview program called The Working Poet Radio Show, filmed live from the Central Library in downtown LA.

**Leonard Nash** received a Florida Book Award Silver Medal for his debut collection, *You Can't Get There from Here and Other Stories* (Kitsune Books, 2007). Nash earned his MFA in Creative Writing from Florida International University. His work has appeared in the *South Dakota Review, The Seattle Review,* the *South Florida Sun-*

*Sentinel, Gulf Stream Magazine, Fort Lauderdale Magazine,* and elsewhere. Nash was born in Miami Beach, grew up in the City of Miami, and now lives in Hollywood, Florida, where he is a freelance writing and editing consultant, and a residential and commercial Realtor. He has taught creative writing at Florida International University and the Florida Center for the Literary Arts at Miami Dade College.

**Melanie Neale** grew up living aboard a 47-foot sailboat with her parents and her sister. The family traveled the US East Coast and the Bahamas from the mid 1980s to the end of the 1990s, and both daughters were home-schooled until they went to college. Melanie began writing poetry and short stories when she was a young child, and she earned a BFA degree in Creative Writing from Eckerd College in 2002 and a MFA degree in Creative Writing from Florida International University in 2006. She lived aboard her own 28-foot sailboat while in graduate school in Miami. She has taught college, captained and crewed on boats, detailed boats, worked in a bait shop, worked in marketing, and currently works as the Director of Career Services for a private art college in northern Florida, where she lives with her husband and daughter. Melanie has published fiction, poetry and nonfiction in many literary journals and magazines, including *Soundings, Seaworthy, Southwinds, GulfStream, Latitudes & Attitudes, The Miami Herald's Tropical Life Magazine, Balancing the Tides, The Georgetown Review, RumBum.com* and *Florida Humanities.* She is also a recipient of several awards for her writing. Her "Short Story" column appeared bimonthly in *Cruising World Magazine* from 2006 to 2009. *Boat Girl: A Memoir of Youth, Love, and Fiberglass* is her first book.

**Ricardo Pau-Llosa** is the author of seven books of poetry, the last five of which have been published by Carnegie Mellon University Press. His work has been widely published in major literary magazines and anthologies. His short stories have also appeared in such magazines as *Fiction* and *New England Review* and in anthologies such as *Sudden Fiction International (Continued),* published by W. W. Norton. He is also an art critic and curator, with a specialty in modern and contemporary Latin American art. More at pau-llosa.com.

**Geoffrey Philp**, author of *Garvey's Ghost* and spokesperson for the Coalition for the Exoneration of Marcus Garvey, teaches English at Miami Dade College, where he also chairs the College Preparatory Department. A critically acclaimed author, he has also won many awards for his poetry and fiction, including a Florida Individual Artist Fellowship, Sauza "Stay Pure" Award, James Michener Fellowships from the University of Miami, and in 2008, he won the coveted "Outstanding Writer " prize from the Jamaica Cultural Development Commission. He maintains a blog at geoffreyphilp. blogspot.com.

A copy editor at the *Tampa Bay Times*, **Ian Vasquez** is the author of three crime novels, *In the Heat*, which won the Shamus Award in 2008, *Lonesome Point* and *Mr. Hooligan*. He holds an MFA from Florida International University in Miami, where he lived, worked and partied for several years—from Coconut Grove to Doral to Kendall to Little Havana. He misses the energy of the city, but not the traffic. He now lives with his family near Tampa, and believes that, yes, Miami does make better Cuban bread than Tampa.